Hooker Daughter

Beggar Father

For: people who deserve a second chance

.

Other Titles by

Andrew S. S. Chan

The Invisible Rings: A Long-distant Love Story
At the Tea House: Where D.S. meets B.S.
Are We Lucky or What
Common Sense for Good Health & Longevity
Mu Mo: The Accidental Monk Golfer

Paperback and E-book are available at Amazon.com, Barnes and Noble, or any other major bookstore.

Acknowledgement

Many thanks to:

My wife – without her trust, magnanimity and sincere encouragement I wouldn't be able to familiarize myself with night ladies and madams and their profession, which is crucial to the authenticity of this book.

Madame Anonymous – for letting me do my research at her "happy house" and for writing a very graceful introduction for this book.

Nightingales of Lake Eleazy – without sharing their personal lives and trade secrets with me my story couldn't be as true and lively as it is.

My golf buddy – without his in-depth local knowledge this book couldn't be as salty and peppery as it is.

Introduction
By Author

You may wonder why a decent man like me who came from a decent family and now has a decent family myself, would want to write a book about a prostitute.

It is purely accidental.

It all began when I had a drink with a friend after a round of golf. He told me a very sad story about his friend whose life had been turned upside down because their only daughter had become a hooker.

After hearing that, I felt sad and the sadness had been lingering on for days. I couldn't imagine how much sadder if she were our daughter. A nice innocent girl who has been raised like a princess turned out to be a hooker! It must have been devastating for her parents! Though we are fortunate not to have this kind of thing happened to us, I can still feel their pains all the same. Dear readers please take a moment, close your eyes, just to imagine, see if you can feel the same pain as I have felt. After thinking how many hookers and devastated parents are there in this world, I decided to write a book about them – to examine and explore the causes – to remind parents that raising children is a huge responsibility besides making, feeding and clothing them.

By Madame X

I'm Madame Anonymous and I run a "happy house" in Lake Eleazy. I want to tell you a very interesting story about how I got to know the author of this book. It was in the evening three years ago, about eight o'clock and shortly after we had opened the door for business, a thin old man with a briefcase came in, looking quite nervous. At that time we had a few girls out there in the lobby, chattering idly while waiting for customers. They thought he was an accountant, came for some fun after a day's boring work at the office, and they nearly got into a fight over him; for old men are generally easy to handle, they tend to be more gentle and generous and they are quick. But to their surprise, he wanted none of them. He wanted to speak to the manager.

When I came out to meet him, the girls were teasing me, thinking he was an old customer of mine. But, I didn't know him and I'd never seen him before. I asked what he wanted and he told me he was an author and he wanted to write a book about a hooker and her father. Write a book about us? No! I'd have screamed and had one of our bouncers to kick him out like a soccer ball if not for his scholarly look and gentlemanly demeanor. Although my profession is low and I am illiterate, I always have high respect for educated people. And I had more for this old gentleman after he had opened his briefcase to show me the five books he had written.

I've met many men in my life, young and old, rich and poor, and from all walks of life, but I've never met one like him. Unlike all the others who'd come to abuse and disgrace us, he came to do research for his new book. He treated us like a fellow human being with respect and kindness. He brought us food and wine and didn't mind a bit to stay to eat with us. At first, we suspected him a phony, like our other customers who wanted to buy our hearts with sweet talks and cheap gifts and expected something in return for free. But time has proved we were wrong. He is a real gentleman and he wants nothing from us. Thank you, Mr. Chan, you've helped us getting our dignity back, and now, we feel like we are normal people again.

ONE

At Stagecoach Inn, a neighborhood coffee shop in Old Town, Tamekola, a group of old-timers squeezed into a long table at the back of the restaurant drinking coffee, reading newspapers, and munching on bacons and eggs. The restaurant is over one hundred years old and is listed as a historical landmark. It used to be a saloon and the only layover for stagecoach passengers traveling north from Escondido to Riverside, where they could spend a night recuperating from a long day of dusty and rocking ride. Now, it is a very popular meeting place for locals and tourists alike. The saloon had long since been converted into a dining area, serving breakfast, lunch and dinner; and the half dozen of rooms upstairs are no longer guest rooms. They had been turned into storage areas for useless junks, and their current tenants are merry mice and restless ghosts.

Most of the old-timers who came every morning, rain or shine, were retirees and lived within a few blocks away. They came to gossip, argue, and recycle some boring news from the only local newspapers. They came not particularly for the food but for the companionship and the friendly atmosphere of the restaurant, where everybody knew each other. For them it was a sanctuary to where they could get away from their nagging old wives for a few hours, and where a few lonely, dirty old men could get their kicks of the day by giving the waitresses a pat on their butts when they were passing by, or by putting in their hands a quarter tip instead of leaving it on the table. As long as they were not trying to force a kiss on them the waitresses normally didn't mind their harmless naughtiness; they felt sorry for them lonely old grandpas and were glad to let them have a little fun.

Routinely they ended their morning gathering in heated arguments and went home mad as hell with each other. But, they all seemed to have poor memories, for by the time they met next morning, they acted like old buddies again.

"Where's Rob these days, I haven't seen him for a while?" an old-timer asked.

"I heard he's sick," replied another old-timer who sat next to him.

"If I were him, I'll be sick, too," said Jay Jensen, a gossipy man who was always the first to come and the last to leave, and he talked the most.

"What's that supposed to mean?" They all asked, sensing there was a piece of sharp chicken bone embedded in his words.

"You guys don't know?" Jay asked, lowering his voice almost to whispering level, and then with pretentious suspension he said, "What a shame, Rob's daughter was seen standing at Three Corner in Lake Eleazy."

"What's she doing there?"

"What else but hustling."

"What! She's a hooker? Who saw her?"

"I don't know. My wife said a friend told her."

"Are you sure it's her? Rob and his wife have only this daughter and they've raised her like a princess; I can't believe she's gotten this low."

"That's the problem," Jay said. "They'd spoiled her. I heard she was a poor student and didn't like to be around good neighboring kids, but loved to hang out with a bunch of no-good boys, and before she even turned fourteen, she was already doing alcohol and drugs. Remember

2

Bobby Stewart's boy, the one who died of overdose two years ago? What's his name—?"

"Johnny."

"Yes, Johnny. He was a pimp and he was the one who got her into porn business. When Rob and his wife had found out, they chewed her up so badly that she ran away from home. And because of her Rob and his wife were in bad terms ever since, quarreling all the time. I was told that her committing suicide had a lot to do with it. I don't know you guys have noticed or not, Rob has changed a great deal. He used to be a very happy man although he didn't talk much. Now, he doesn't come here as often and when he did come he looked sad. I really feel sorry for him."

"How come you know so much and we know nothing?"

"I have a pair of good ears," answered Jay smugly.

"You got a big mouth too," mocked Randy Gibbs. He never liked Jay much solely because Jay had a bad mouth, gossiping like a long-tongued old maid. Now, Randy was upset because Jay was talking about his good neighbor behind his back and seemed to enjoy every minute of it.

Everyone knew Randy was not joking and they sealed their lips immediately. Only Jack Musk, a real, real old old-timer, did not get the message. Perhaps, he didn't hear what Randy said because his hearing was either very poor or his brain couldn't digest it fast enough, he said, "I know his wife had passed away last year and we all went to her funeral. Boy, what a funeral! Rob was mad like hell when his daughter showed up. He hollered at her and chased her out like a mad dog. I was wondering what his daughter had done to make him that angry. By the way, Jay, why didn't you tell us this before?"

3

Jay took a glance at Randy's unpleasant face and felt uneasy to talk about Rob Taylor's daughter anymore. He decided to ignore Jack Musk's untimely question.

"Didn't you hear me, Jay? I asked you a question!" Old Musk asked again in much louder voice, not getting the message that Jay had intentionally ignored him.

"Could I tell you when Rob was here?" answered Jay reluctantly as he saw from the corners of his eyes that Randy was watching him. He was smart enough not to aggravate him further.

Randy had been listening disturbingly; for he knew what Jay had said about Rob's daughter was very credible, though he disapproved his spreading the rumor. He had been Rob Taylor's next-door neighbor for more than thirty years and they were close friends and had spent a lot of time together, especially after the death of their wives. Whatever happened in Rob's household Randy and his wife knew. They saw them play and heard them laugh when their daughter was young, but as she grew older, they heard scolding and quarrels instead. They had been long suspecting Rob's daughter was in trouble, first with school and then with alcohol and drugs, but they never knew she was involved in porno movies and prostitution, too. It was a bombshell for him! Damn you, Rob, why didn't you tell me about this? We're good friends, he complained silently.

Naturally, Rob didn't tell him because they seldom talked about personal and family matters, for Randy was truly a gentleman and he didn't like to pry on other people's personal business; and Rob was an introvert, not a gossipy person. The only time he would open his mouth was when he was asked how to fix a gadget, otherwise, he would be content to be a silent listener.

4

Jay was not the only one that had upset Randy, the bad news of Rob's daughter was more unsettling. Randy and his wife had been watching her growing up and treating her like their own daughter. Hearing her now was a hooker gave him indigestion. Another concern he had was Rob; he worried if Rob was really sick. Being sick and alone is a miserable combination. He knew, for he had been sick many times since his wife had passed away five years ago, and every time he felt sicker when there was no one came to help or to comfort. "Why didn't you tell me?" he grumbled aloud in frustration on his way home. "I thought we're good friends and I must have to learn about this from other people?"

TWO

Came back from Breakfast Randy saw Rob's car parked in front of the garage at exactly the same spot as it was for the last three days. It was apparent that Rob had not gone anywhere during that time. For a moment, he was tempted to knock on Rob's door to see if he was all right, but he changed his mind, for he had done that several times already the day before and there was no answer. Maybe he doesn't want to see me, he thought. Dejected, he turned around and walked back to his house. "But why, we're good friends," he talked to himself again, wondering why Rob wanted to avoid him and told him nothing. "Well, he may have his reasons and, besides, this is a very personal matter; he may not want anyone to know. If I were him, I probably would've done the same thing."

But, he couldn't stop worrying about his good neighbor. He had had enough despondent experience to know how dreadful it was to be sick and live alone, and how desperate for someone to call, to show concern, to offer help. He could still remember vividly how helpless and sad he was when he couldn't care for himself and there was no one came to help. After another round of mental tuck-of-wars, he decided to give Rob a call.

There was no answer after many rings, which made Randy worry all the more and he began imagining all sorts of things that might have happened to Rob. "Where could he be?" He talked to himself again. He had been talking to himself a lot ever since the death of his wife, for he was living alone and had no one to talk to. "He doesn't have many friends and he can't be out shopping for his car is here. Is he seriously sick or he has committed suicide just like his wife did? Oh, no! It's quite possible if he's learned about his daughter is a hooker. Not many lonely old folks can withstand such a jolt, and Rob is old and lonely and he hasn't shown up for breakfast at Stagecoach Inn for three days already." The more he thought about the remote but disheartening possibility, the more worrisome he became, so worrisome that he couldn't sit still. With shaking fingers he punched in the numbers again and this time he let the phone ring continuously until he heard Rob's lethargic voice on the other end.

"Hello, who's it?"

"This is me, Randy. Are you okay, my friend? You sound awful!"

"Yes, I'm not feeling well."

"What's it? Have you gone see a doctor?" Randy knew the answer already but he asked anyway.

"No, it's nothing serious, only a minor headache."

"Have you had breakfast yet?"

"No. I'm not hungry."

"I'll get you something to eat. I'll be right over." Randy hung up and gave Rob no chance to say no. With his worry completely gone, he said aloud, "Thanks God, he's not dead!"

With Rob's favorite breakfast from Stagecoach Inn, Randy knocked at Rob's door half an hour later, and when it was opened the stench of alcohol and tobacco rushed into his nostrils. It was so strong that he subconsciously stepped back and covered his nose with his idle right hand. Only then, he was stunned by the sickening look of Rob and by what he saw behind him: all over the place were empty liquor bottles, cigarette butts, newspapers, magazines and old photos. Rob's living room looked like a back alley in a slum. He had never ever seen Rob or his house look like this before! And Rob was not a heavy drinker and he seldom smoked.

Rob Taylor used to be an electrical engineer and he was always neat and tidy and did things meticulously. As a widower he kept his house cleaner and tidier than most decent housewives. Now, he looked like a night owl with two black rings around his eyes and was unshaved, and probably had not brushed his teeth for days, for they were yellowish with stains.

"Here, I've brought you something to eat," said Randy as he looked at his friend with disbelief. "You look like you need some real food in your stomach."

"Thanks. But I'm not hungry."

"You must eat something, Rob, unless you really want to kill yourself. Say, what's the matter with you, getting yourself so drunk?"

Trying to evade Randy's pressing questions; Rob was busily opening the containers of food with no intention of eating any of it. But the aroma of steaming coffee, the smell of bacon, and the sight of a thick pile of blueberry pancakes with a big slab of butter on top and maple syrup cascading down their sides, had suddenly made him a very hungry man. He gorged on the food like a beggar at a feast until the Styrofoam plate and cup were as clean as new.

"Now, tell me what had happened to you," asked Randy again the moment Rob had finished his breakfast with a tone so firm that it was almost like a command, which made any attempt of further evasion impossible.

"It's Angie again; she's shamed our family. She'd killed her mother and now she wants to kill me, too. All these years since she left home, I assumed she was dead. I'd almost forgotten all about her and I was doing fine.

But now, she's a whore and the whole town knows. How can I go out there to face friends and neighbors? I feel like—like a whore myself. Do you understand, Randy?" Rob poured out his grievances and frustrations in torrents, like a dam had been cracked opened suddenly. He had been carrying the load alone and nobody came to lighten it, and the pain and suffering became unbearable. He was desperate in need of a listener on whom he could unload. "I don't understand why she'd turned out like this; we've tried our best to raise her good. We're not rich but we've deprived her nothing; we gave her everything she ever wanted and she was a princess in our family. Now, she's a..." Rob was shaking his head despondently and started sobbing. A few drops of old tears running down his wrinkled cheeks.

Randy was speechless. In a situation like this it was very difficult to find the right words to say. At length, he said, "Don't blame yourself, Rob; it's not your fault. We have no children ourselves but I know it isn't easy to raise kids nowadays, too much outside influence."

"No, we are responsible for Angie's downfall. I still remember you'd warned us when Angie was still a toddler..."

"If I did I don't remember."

"Yes, you did and you said we should be careful with Angie, don't give her too much attention, for it might end up spoiling her. I hate myself now that I didn't take your advice seriously. But Angie was so lovely then, it was hard not to love her and spoil her a little. Of course, if we knew then, that our excessive love would've eventually ruined her, we'd have been more careful about it. Now, it's too late. It's our fault, we've destroyed her."

"Don't be too hard on yourself; you're not alone, many parents have made the same mistake."

9

"I don't care about Angie anymore, she's hurt us enough and Mary had died because of her. But, I do care about my dignity. I just don't feel comfortable going out any more, people will talk. I've been thinking about moving out of here, to some place nobody knows me so that I can live in peace."

"Even want to get away from your friends and neighbors of thirty years? Don't be silly, Rob! Let people talk, why should you care? If they're really your friends, they won't talk and they'll help you get over it instead. By the way, I'm curious, from whom you learned about this?

"I overheard Jay's wife telling two other women at Wholesome Food Mart. You know she talks mighty loud and I was happened to be in the next aisle."

"Oh, that gossipy couple again, I don't like them! Jay told everybody at Stagecoach Inn this morning and that's why I know."

Rob Taylor said nothing, only shaking his head continuously, showing his disapproval. He was greatly disappointed by Jay Jensen whom he thought was his friend. He had helped him fixing so many things over the years.

"Are you sure Angie is in that business?" asked Randy suddenly.

"What do you mean? You don't suppose they made it up, do you?"

"It's hard to say; it is only a rumor, it may not be true."

"I have no reason to doubt what people say. Angie is a bad girl. What else she wouldn't do?"

"Still, I think you should check it out, just to make sure."

"How, go to watch her hustling?"

"That's exactly what I have in mind. That's the only way we can be sure. How about driving up there tonight?"

"You must be out of your mind. You don't worry me shooting her down like a dog if I should see her...? Do you have any idea how much it'd hurt to see your own daughter doing that? Of course, you don't! You have no daughter!"

"I do! Believe me, I do!" said Randy passionately. Since he and his wife had no children they had regarded Angie as their own daughter, and that was why he had dispensed some advice to Rob out of concern. "But you must find a way to save her. She's your daughter, for God's sake!"

"No, I don't want to save her," said Rob resolutely. "Nobody can save her now. She's beyond help!"

"Come on, Rob, you don't mean that and I know you don't! You aren't that kind of a guy. Go, have a good rest. You look awful. I'll be back around six; we'll have dinner in Lake Eleazy tonight. I know a good Italian restaurant there." Randy left without waiting for Rob to say "Yes" or "No."

Rob could not rest; he was torn to pieces by so many contradictory thoughts. He really did not want to find out whether the rumor was true or not. It made no difference to him, for the damage caused by his daughter's shameful occupation had already been done. It was much easier to assume it was true and assume he never had such a daughter. It took him a long time to gradually erase her from his mind, and his life had yet got back to normal completely. He definitely wouldn't allow anything to derail the progress. But, to refuse Randy's help was ill-disposed. He was his best friend and was the wisest man he knew; he might be able to save his daughter from drowning. The thought of saving his daughter sparked a light of hope and rekindled the pile of cold ash inside him. How wonderful it will be if she can really change and be-

11

come our little princess again, and how pleasing if she'll get married and settle down and live a normal life, he thought. The memory of his lovely princess began dancing and smiling innocently before him. But the memory of her defiance and disrespect at their last squabble, her running away from home, and his wife's untimely death had brought back a chilling effect that disheartened him tremendously.

While Rob was lying in bed fighting his internal war, Randy went to Sports Park to take his daily walk. Normally, he did it at the small city park near his home, but today he wanted to be in a place quieter so that he could do some serious thinking. The small city park was just too busy for him not to be distracted.

He walked leisurely and aimlessly, but his brain was working feverishly on a feasible plan to save his best friend's daughter.

THREE

Shortly after six Randy came and spent more than five minutes waiting for Rob to open the door. The doorbell had waked him up. Two days of heavy drinking to drown off his sorrows had worn him out and a big breakfast had made him drowsy.

"Have a good nap?" Randy asked. "Let's go get something to eat."

"You go, I'm not hungry." Rob was hungry all right, a good, long sleep had restored his appetite, but he did not want to chance seeing his daughter standing at street corners. He wasn't sure he could control himself emotionally; he might do something irrational and horrible.

"Come on, let's go. Don't argue with me!" Randy gave order. He was four years older than Rob and he always acted like an older brother to him.

After they had ordered their dinners and two pots of hot tea, Rob asked, "Tell me, why Lake Eleazy got such a bad reputation?"

"Don't you know," Randy looked at Rob incredulously. "This town is the murder and porno capital of the country."

"No kidding, who told you that?"

"It has the highest murder rate in the country and many of the adult movies are made here."

"How do you know?" Rob asked the same question again. He had to find out the city where his daughter worked was really that dangerous. He wouldn't admit it but, somehow, he was still concerned about her safety.

"I used to have my office here and I often went to the local bars with colleagues after work. You know, that was

13

what we did to entertain ourselves when we were young and single. I met all kinds of people there, after a few drinks their tongues were loose and they talked freely. I acquired a lot of information that way."

"Now, tell me why they have so many murders here."

"Well, to answer your question, you have to know the history of this town. You see, it was a very small, quiet town then, there was no freeway coming here until the early eighty, only a poorly maintained highway that nobody used except the locals and a few low-budgeted vacationers who came to swim and fish in the lake. Once, a dreamer wanted to develop it into another Palm Springs to attract the Hollywood sets to come for its beautiful lake and many natural hot springs. He built a casino hotel perched on a small hill overlooking a magnificent lake and distant mountain ranges to the west. The hotel had a grand ballroom elegantly designed for dancing, a fine-dining restaurant, and a couple of bars and, of course, a gaming area. It had also seventeen luxurious rooms and five of them had their own private pools filled with natural spring water. He also brought in a huge flat-bottomed boat, floating in the lake, offering lunch and dinner cruises on weekends and holidays. With hundreds of multicolored decorative lights glimmering, playing rivalry to the millions of twinkling midsummer-night stars, and the Big Band music playing, it was surely a very romantic and relaxing place to be. It was a great idea; his novelty resort had attracted a lot of weekenders, even a few big-named movie stars, from Los Angeles and the surrounding coastal cities. But after about a year or so doing fantastic business, the lake refused to cooperate with him; it dried up after years of drought and his fancy boat sitting on mud at the bottom of the lake, and tons of stinking dead fish gave the lake its first bad reputation – the Stinking Lake. When you mentioned Lake Eleazy people would frown and pinch their noses, and they still do but the stinking is now not from dead fish but from murders, prostitution, and pornography.

"This city's bad name had turned away a lot of ordinary people and developments even after the completion of the remaining stretch of Freeway 15 between Corona and Escondido. For the same reason it drew in hundreds and thousands of welfare recipients from the big cities because of its cheap housings and remoteness. Living here and claiming they did not own a car, they could receive their welfare checks in the mail without going through the hassles of picking them up from the welfare offices, and could also avoid the mandatory job interviews. With government money and all the time in the world, what else would they do or could do but drinking, doing drugs, and making babies.

"Due to cheap housings, abundant supply of eager wannabe actors and actresses, and easier to get to because of Freeway 15, Lake Eleazy has become the porn capital of the world where most adult videos are filmed, where porn stars, hookers, drug pushers and drug addicts inhabit. It is not hard to distinguish them from the rest of the population; porn stars are physically fit and dress provocatively, hookers look almost the same except they are older and out of shape, and most of them are former porn stars. To the untrained eyes drug pushers and drug addicts look like ordinary people; only they, themselves, can recognize each other.

"I feel sorry for the children who are growing up here in such an environment, do you think they have the desire going to college and having a decent job? No. Most of them end up like their parents – welfare recipients. Some ambitious and enterprising young people go into business to make extra money to support their addictive habits. But, with no skills and educations all they can do is pimping and selling drugs."

Rob had been listening attentively; the city's history was quiet interesting and Randy's analysis made a lot of sense to him except the very last part, of which he felt a little offended. "I guess we're lousy parents like those welfare recipients; we hadn't been giving our child a proper environment to grow up." But the tone he said it with was quiet negative, clearly resentful.

"Sorry, Rob. It seems to me I've offended you, but I didn't mean it that way. I was talking about Lake Eleazy in the old days, certainly not in your case. You and your wife had been giving your daughter a very warm and loving home; she had all the opportunities any child from a good family could have. Angie just had the wrong kind of friends, that's all."

"It's our fault, no denial about that! We weren't smart enough to foresee the troubles ahead; we thought her friends were a bunch of fun-loving kids and would be all right eventually when they grew up." Rob's tone was much pleasanter; he regretted he had been too sensitive to get angry with his best friend.

"Who's that smart and never makes a mistake? We all make some mistakes one way or the other." Randy said and then he changed the subject casually. "I've been doing some thinking this afternoon and I think I've figured out a way to get Angie out of this nasty business—"

"Save your breath, I'm not interested," interrupted Rob.

"Why, you can't be serious, she's your daughter!" asked Randy, stunned. He had not expected Rob would react so negatively. Refusing help to save his daughter?

16

"Don't force me, please. I don't want to have anything to do with her, period!"

"I want to know why you're so determined, if you don't mind."

"Why? You'll know why if you'd heard what she said to us the night she ran away."

"Oh, really that bad you can't forgive her? What did she say to make you so?"

"Five years ago when we found out she was in adult movie business, Mary and I were devastated; our princess in dirty movies and let the whole world watch! When I told her either to quit or move out, she shouted at me: 'What's wrong with my job, I make more money in a day than you do in a month.' I said, 'You don't call selling your body and soul a job. A plumber's job is cleaner than yours!' The pugnacious daughter of ours yelled back: 'What's the difference! Mama sold her body and soul to you for a long-termed meal ticket and you sold yours to your boss for a lousy salary. Every time your boss needs you, you have to go. You couldn't even wait until I finished cutting my birthday cake, remember?' Have you ever heard of such a daughter so disrespectful to her parents? Do you know how badly she'd hurt us? We're so hurt and angry that Mary slapped her and I ordered her out of the house."

Randy was flabbergasted. He couldn't believe any person, no matter how bad they are, dare to insult their parents like this, using such a horrible language. But he knew it was true; Rob wouldn't lie to him. Finally he said, trying to placate his fuming friend, "Angie was young, like most young people who don't know how to talk to their parents; she just burst out when she was mad. I'm sure she didn't mean it. And possibly, she could have un-

17

der the influence at that time, too; I heard Johnny Stewart was a drug addict. He might get her hooked…"

"I can forgive her for what she'd said to us, but I can't forgive her for what she'd done to her mother. She was the one who had driven Mary to her death."

"I know Mary would if she were still alive. Mothers never have any acrimony with their children for long. I hate to say it, but you and Mary should bear some of the blames for Angie's bad conducts. You folks had really pampered her by giving her whatever she wanted and by treating her like a high princess. Children need guidance and discipline from parents besides love. I know, I have no children myself and am not in a position to give advice on how to raise them. But I saw our neighbors, the Lee, the Valenzuela, and the Goldsmith, they're not rich but they gave their children guidance and worked them hard. Look at their children now; they're all nice and success-ful, too."

Rob was silent; he couldn't find words to argue. What Randy had said was all true. They were his neigh-bors, too, and he knew them as well as Randy did. Their children were about the same age as his daughter, but, in-stead of letting them hanging out at theaters and malls, they got them jobs at McDonald's. Instead of letting them watching TV and on the phone with friends for hours, they made them mow lawns and wash dishes. And instead of dressing them like princesses and princes, they bought books and computers for them. He had to admit that he and his wife had ruined their daughter and her turning bad was their own fault. And he knew, too, that his wife would have forgiven Angie a thousand times if she were still alive. All she needed was an insincere apology or a deceitful hug from her daughter. Thinking about his wife's tragic death brought back the guilt and remorse.

Only if I had taken some of the responsibilities and not put all the blames on her, she might not have killed herself, it was my blaming her, the last straw, that had killed her, he thought.

"Tell me how we can save her," he asked Randy reticently, indicating he was willing to listen.

When Randy told him his plan which required him to be a beggar, he was dismayed and he said, "You want me to act like a beggar and sit on the sidewalk to beg? You must be kidding! Do you know how shameful it is to be a beggar? And me, a respectful engineer has turned into a beggar? What will our friends and neighbors think of me? What about my dignity, my pride? No, thank you! I can't do it!"

"I think you must, Rob, for this is the only way I could think of that might be able to touch Angie, to stir up her emotion. I think she still carries a guilty conscience for her mother's death and she still loves you and won't stand seeing you beg. I bet she'll come to me for help and then, I'll convince her to come home. Just to image your Angie becoming a good girl again and Mary will be very pleased in her grave, Rob."

"She, my good girl again, don't be dreaming, Randy. I've never heard of any alcoholic or drug addicts can become clean again, have you?"

"You'll be surprised. It won't cost you anything to try anyway."

"It won't cost you but will cost me a lot! What about my face? People, they—they'd talk!" Rob was still not feeling comfortable about the whole thing.

"Look at it this way, Rob; it'll give you a chance to find out who your real friends are and who aren't."

Rob was thinking hard for a moment before he said reluctantly, "All right, let's give it a try to see if it works."

FOUR

After dinner, they drove a few blocks to Three Corner which was the notorious spot in Lake Eleazy, famous for its dubious activities after dark. It was a small place at the intersection of two streets, all it had were a gas station, a small market, a dirty restaurant, a convenient store and a sleazy drugstore that its fastest moving items were condoms and syringes. There was nothing at the southwestern corner but a slice of dirty beach littered with beer cans, wine bottles, empty cigarette boxes, used syringes, and all sorts of junks. It did have a beautiful lake view though if you could ignore the trashes and the foul smells.

They parked the car at a good distance away from Three Corner – far enough not to be seen but close enough to observe all the activities that happened there. It was a hot and muggy midsummer night and the air was suffocating. They rolled the windows all the way down and sat inside the car watching.

At eight o'clock, Three Corner, the infamous promenade for carnal pleasure seekers and the farmer's market for night hawkers, was deplorably empty and quiet. It was still too early for the creepy night people to appear but too late and dangerous for ordinary citizens to be out in the streets. Not until after nine o'clock that night people started crawling out onto the streets from their underground burrows like snarls and slugs after a rainstorm, crowding in groups at all three street corners and the reeking little beach across Lakeside Drive from them. If the dark and filthy beach was the choice place for drug deals and other illegal activities, Three Corner was the hot spot for night hawkers to display their merchandise, hookers to hook their starving "johns" with charms and meaty bodies, and pimps to show off their flashy cars and outrageous outfits.

The two nervous investigators had been sitting in the car for a long time, watching, trying to calm down their nerves and kill the time with small talks. They could have taken a walk around the blocks but they thought it would be too risky. They didn't want to be spotted by someone they knew, to start a rumor about them paying a visit to Three Corner at night; the embarrassment alone would have been too much for them let alone the damage it would have done to their good reputations.

By ten o'clock, Three Corner was as busy as a Japanese fish market at three o'clock in the morning; myriad of noises filled the air and voices buzzed like there was a huge colony of bees. The night ladies dressed themselves as hot as the steaming ground they stood on; their hot pants were almost as short as their panties and as tight as the black stockings they were wearing. And because it was a warm and clammy night, most of them bared their upper body save a piece of cloth barely covered their breasts. Although very few of them had actually gone to college, much less had taken a marketing class; they were marketing experts, doing an excellent job displaying their wares. They learned it on the job. The midnight cowboys were good at marketing, too; they sported outrageous outfits in the latest fashion and they weren't shy to show them off.

But the food market was the center of attraction; there were no less than a dozen of makeshift food stands on both sides of Lakeside Drive, selling all kinds of ethnic foods, from Mexican to Vietnamese and from hot-dog to ramen. It was the air, the noise, the people, and the confusing atmosphere that made Three Corner a truly melting pot, which attracted people from as far as San Diego and

Los Angles. It was not the cheap food they came for but for a lot more expensive stuffs sold on the side. Although Lake Eleazy was small and relatively poor, there was no shortage of entrepreneurs. Half a dozen of pot farmers were growing their money plants in pots inside covered patios and selling them at their hot dog stands for five bucks a joint. Two retired chemists working as partners had turned their two-car garage into a state-of-the-art laboratory, inventing a long list of effective drugs. If their inventions were for curing people instead of killing people, they probably would've won the Nobel Prize. There were many more talented entrepreneurs and adventurous pioneers in this chaotic city, such as part-time moonshiners, little-foot masseuses, hourly-rate-hotel operators, temporary marriage brokers, and criminal protection agencies, just to mention a few.

But, none of them were more endowed than Hot Pepper, who single-handedly had built a thriving business out of a common vegetable – hot pepper. He cultivated different varieties of hot peppers from around the world and his most prized one was a Chinese pepper called Pointing-at-the-sky. This little, concrete-nail-shaped red pepper not only is one of the hottest pepper in the world but also grows very strangely – instead of hanging down with its tip pointing downward like all other peppers, its tip points at the sky, and that is how it got its name and its reputation as a potent sex-enhancer. The Chinese had discovered it and *believed* in it for thousands of years. So did Hot Pepper when he was doing some research on various peppers. Hot Pepper had a logical mind because he got a degree in horticulture, but it had long been polluted by the environment he lived in. He was thinking about sex and money all the time. Quite naturally, when he was thinking about them and the reputation of this Pointing-at-the-sky

Chinese hot pepper and the six-billion strong Chinese, he put them together and came up with a hot product, selling like hot cakes under the name called what else but HPSE (stand for Hot Pepper Sex Enhancer). It was, however, the way Hot Pepper marketed his cheap HPSE that showed his real talent; he was not selling hot peppers as they are in supermarkets, but drying them, grounding them up into powder form, mixing them with other secret ingredients – brown sugar and peppermint extract for taste and two kinds of Chinese herbs for secrecy – and packaging them into small individual packages, with a label read: *Don't try it at home!*

His generic Viagra made him a millionaire and they were sold everywhere in this notorious city – in drug-stores, grocery stores, hotels, massage parlors, whore-houses, and public restrooms through vending machines. Even hookers carried them to make extra money on the side. Is HPSE effective as it claims? It all depends on whom you ask; the persons who'd used it at a whorehouse or in an hourly-rate hotel room would more likely say yes, but the persons who had ignored the warning label and tried it at home would definitely say no. Only Hot Pepper himself understood the secret and he often said, "Even a dead wood will burn in an inferno but will remain dead in a freezer."

After eleven o'clock, there was still no sign of his daughter and Rob Taylor was relieved. He could now breathe much easier, for his worry of losing his cool and of acting impulsively and violently should he witness her hustling had gone. Thanks God, it's only a rumor, he thought. But, if she's not a hooker, what's she and where's she? She may be still in the movie business or very sick from heroin addiction or may have died of over-dose just like her ex-boyfriend, Johnny Stewart. The grim thoughts made him sick of worrying once more. Now, he wasn't sure if he would like to see his daughter appear tonight or would like to never ever see her again.

They waited in silence but with high anxiety.

"Hey, here she comes," whispered Randy suddenly and it aroused Rob from his distant thoughts – mostly unpleasant thoughts of the past, of the many ugly quarrels he and his wife had with his daughter, and of the exchanges of blames and hurtful words that he believed was the cause of his wife's death.

Following the direction of Randy's eyes, Rob saw his daughter walking toward a group of hookers in front of the convenient store, chattering and laughing. Being only recently demoted from porn star, she was the sexiest and prettiest among them, and with her six-inch high heels she was the tallest one, too. She wore a pair of white booty shorts and a cut-off white T-shirt which not only strategically exposed her somewhat flat belly but also part of her breasts. She was almost too beautiful to be a hooker and yet, not young and attractive enough to remain in the movie business. Her breasts and belly had shown signs of aging and her face had lost the youthful luster. She had maintained her charm though, that was one of the reasons she commanded a premium price and was the most sought-after hooker in town.

Now, more cars rolled into Three Corner and they slowed down in front of the nightingales and night hawkers, gawking, chattering, flirting, laughing, bargaining, and creating an instant traffic jam. Some picked up a girl and some picked up a package. But Angie remained standing on the sidewalk, unsold. Obviously not many "johns" could afford her price. Suddenly, a black limo pulled up and stopped in front of her, and after she had been talking to the driver through the roll-down window for a few minutes, she got in and it sped away.

Rob was watching with deep emotion, an emotion that made his chest heaving like tidal waves and his eye balls riding on them like struggling surfers. "Very sad," said Rob in a crackled voice. "She was our princess not so long ago; we handled her with utmost care and tenderness as if she were a piece of most delicate porcelain. But now, she is everybody's whore! For a few dollars she let any filthy and dirty and ugly pig climb on top of her, abuse her and make her do anything they want her to..." Rob broke down and sobbed. Tonight's experience was too much for him to withstand.

"Let's go home," said Randy somberly. He was just as sad as Rob and couldn't bear seeing anymore.

On their way home, none of them said anything. They had nothing more to say. A picture is worth a thousand words and they had seen *enough* pictures tonight. Good-night was the only word they said to each other before they parted.

"What a mess I've made!" Rob shouted when he stepped into his house, not sure he referred to the demise of his daughter or the mess he had made to his house. Stale alcoholic smell rushed into his nostrils and a chaotic mess met his eyes. He was shock that he, an engineer who was immaculate all his life, could live in such a despicable condition for the past three days. Now, after having seen too many filthy and ugly things in one night, he couldn't tolerate the current condition of his house any longer. It had become an eyesore and a good cleanup was almost a must. It not only will make the house more livable but also will enable me to forget what I saw tonight at Three Corner, at least for a while, he thought.

25

While he was cleaning and tidying and putting things back to where they belonged, his mind could not help but wander back to find fault with himself. "Why, why we did this to our daughter? Perhaps Randy is right, we did spoil her. Look at Joe's two daughters, they didn't nearly have what Angie had but they both have graduated and have good jobs. David's girl too, she turned out pretty decent even though she didn't go to college. Of all our neighbor's kids, why is she the only one that turns out to be so disappointing?"

By two o'clock in the morning Rob had finished getting his house in good order, but his mind remained just as clustered and chaotic as his house just a few hours ago. He doubted his becoming a beggar would really help saving his daughter. If she doesn't feel ashamed being a hooker, why should she feel ashamed of me being a beggar? And if Randy's idea doesn't work, why should I try it and subject myself to ridicule and humiliation? But, what if Randy is right? He's the smartest man I know and he is seldom wrong about things. And Mary will be groaning and turning in her grave if I don't even give it a try. The thought of not doing it for his wife because of his selfish pride bothered him a lot. "Oh, Mary, Mary, what a monster we've created," he lamented. "But for you, I'll do it. I promise." He swore aloud to reinforce his commitment. At that very moment he decided to do it no matter how painful and embarrassing.

FIVE

A week later, with Randy's help and coaching, Rob was ready to assume his new role as a beggar. He hadn't shaved for ten days now and had let his hair grow wild, which was not an easy task for a neat and clean man like him. He selected a pair of black jeans and a grey T-shirt from a bag of old clothes that he had been saving for Salvation Army, and cut some holes in them to make them look deplorable. He smeared a pair of not-so-old tennis shoe with mud so they looked old. But he refused to obey Randy's order to dirty his face with grease.

But, after he had changed into the beggar outfit and looked at himself in the mirror, the unfamiliar face with a walrus mustache and a sea lion whisker made him sick if his wrinkled clothes and dirty shoes failed to do so. He screamed with horror. "Look at me! How absurd! I can't do it—I just can't do it!"

Randy looked at Rob, grinning, with a mixed feeling of sympathy and guilt, for Rob looked so ridiculous in this meticulously prepared outfit that he nearly burst out with laughter. How could I be so crazy to make a neat man like Rob to look like that – half beggar and half lunatic – he thought apologetically?

For a whole week their plan had been put on hold; Randy went to Stagecoach Inn for the morning gathering as usual and Rob stayed home nursing his anguish alone with something much stronger than beers. During this period, Randy had not come over to Rob's house, for he knew it would be useless trying to change Rob's mind. I mustn't force my idea on him, he thought. It might not work anyway and, after all, she's not my daughter.

27

And Rob, due to heavy drinking and erratic eating in a desperate attempt to ease his misery, let his house go to hell again. One evening, after gazing at the picture of his proud wife holding their baby daughter in front of the hospital where their daughter was born, he broke down, sobbing. Although the picture was taken long, long time ago, it still never failed to stir up his feeling of excitement and happiness every time he saw it. Already half-drunk, he finished the other half bottle of Wild Turkey, hoping the potent stuff would help numb his feeling and put him to sleep and it did before he could finish the last drop. He fell on the couch on his back and the bottle came off his hand, rolling on the floor.

After a long period of silence and inactivity, Rob heard someone knocking at the door, not loud but conveyed a sense of urgency. He staggered to open the door and felt a chill draft before he saw a figure covered in white from head to toe.

"Who're you? What do you want?" He asked apprehensively, his voice trembling. He could not see the face very well for it was as white as the hood it was in.

"I'm your wife! Can't you recognize me, Old Fool?" answered the figure in white.

"You—Mary…?" Rob stuttered. He was stunned more than surprised. He recoiled into the house as if he had been pushed back by a gust of cold wind, and his wife followed him in.

"Why, why you—you come back to see me?" Rob asked timorously after he had steadied himself in an armchair.

"I came to ask you to do me a big favor."

"Why, what's it? You know I'll do anything for you."

"I want you to save Angie. She's in hot oven, suffering," said Rob's wife very calmly.

"You want me to save her? Why, Mary? You'd for-gotten she'd broken your heart and caused you to kill yourself?"

"No, I didn't forget but I forgive her. It wasn't entire-ly her fault; it was ours, too. We'd raised her wrong. Now, we must help her."

"No! I can't forgive her! She called us whores, sell-ing our bodies and souls, yours to me and mine to my boss."

"She's young then and didn't know better. We adults shouldn't take those childish words seriously."

"No, Mary. I won't do it! Please don't force me. You know I was willing to do anything for you and I still do, but not this one."

"Oh, please Rob, I beg you."

"I said no! No is no. If you want to help her, go ahead, help her yourself. It was you who'd spoiled her; otherwise, she wouldn't have turned out to be that bad a girl." By now, Rob had forgotten the person he was talk-ing to was a ghost and, therefore, he showed his old form as a commanding husband.

"I spoiled her? What about you?" Rob's ghost wife suddenly energized by his unfriendly remarks; her white face turned crimson, her voice became loud and piercing, and she moved her hands like a fencing champion, using a lot of prodding and jabbing. "Who's the one always on her side when I tried to discipline her? Who's the one al-ways gave her what she wanted? Have you ever say no to her even you knew I had? Now, you blame it all on me!" The ghost was mad, shrieking and pointing fingers at Rob.

"Stop!" shouted Rob. "Who bought her all the expen-sive brand-named clothes and dressed her like a model? Who took her to the salon, ignoring my objection, to have her manicure done? When I refused to buy her a smart phone, you secretly bought her one, saying: 'All her friends have one, so she'd have one.' When I told her to spend less time hanging around with bad kids and more time on her study, you rushed in to her defense, saying: 'Career is not important for girls but hooking a rich husband is.' Now, she's a good hooker, thanks for your teaching. I bet she can hook a few fish every night. Are you happy now?"

"Stop, for Christ sake, stop!" shouted his ghost wife, throwing up both hands to plug her ears. "You ungrateful bastard, are you implying that I had hooked you, too? Hooking you for the lousy living you provide? What about me, working my butt off for you and getting no pay because you own me? Don't you think you'd hurt me enough when I was alive, and now you want to hurt me more when I'm dead?" Then, she started to cry. Rob had heard his wife cry before, many times, and he hated it. It always made him feel guilty and it never failed to shut him up at once. But his wife's cry as a human compared to her cry as a ghost now was music in his ears. Her cry now was horrifyingly intolerable; it made all his hairs stand on their feet and he felt freezing as if he was inside a walk-in freezer naked.

As always, Rob was silent when his wife got really mad. He loved her too much not to yield to her to avoid a real confrontation. He was more so now that he regretted he had used too strong and hurtful words to attack a ghost, not his Old Mary. He knew what his wife was capable to do as a human, but not quite sure what she would do to him as a ghost. He was afraid that she might drag him underground with her.

Also, as always when she was alive, Rob's ghost wife stopped crying and remained quiet as well. It was an indication for peace, for reconciliation. It was the time to re-member how much and how long they'd loved each other. It was the time to cool down, to amend, and to work as a team.

The cooling period was long and it was Rob's ghost wife that broke the silence first because she was less tenacious than her engineer husband. She pleaded earnestly in a syrupy voice as she was pulling his arm vigorously, "Do this for me, just this once. Please! I won't have rest down there unless our princess is saved."

"I said no! Please don't push me," cried Rob, fighting to free himself from her persistent pulling. He was indeed a very determined man, always stood by his belief and seldom wavered.

"Please...please...Rob..." His wife kept on pleading and pulling and would not stop.

Suddenly, Rob felt he was being pulled off a cliff and falling like a rock...Bang! He hit the ground. He fell off the couch, hitting the floor head first. The fall woke him up instantly and now he realized it was only a bad dream.

"Why, why the dream was so real? Why Mary came to beg me at this time of all times, and told me 'I won't have rest down there unless our princess is saved', which is exactly what Randy had said the other day that Mary would have been if I don't save Angie." Rob was talking to himself aloud, perplexed by the dream and was feeling extremely uncomfortable. Being an engineer he was not a superstitious man, he would normally have dismissed this kind of ghost's visit as a bad dream. But not this time, the timing of his dead wife's visit and the planned saving of his hooker daughter was so strangely close that he could not ignore it as such. So strange that it can't be a coincident, he thought.

He wanted to call Randy over to tell him his dream, it was only ten o'clock and he knew Randy was still up, for he could see, through his living room window, the light was still on. But he changed his mind, for he suddenly realized how messy his house was and his breath was laden with the vile odor of alcohol. It would be embarrassingly disgraceful to face anybody in this condition, even if he was a good neighbor. He had no desire going back to sleep now, lest his ghost wife would pay him another visit. Instead, he spent the rest of the night cleaning up his house until he was too tired to worry about another nightmare.

SIX

When Randy came home after having breakfast at Stagecoach Inn, he saw Rob getting out of his car which was parked outside the garage, and he hailed him: "Morning, Rob, been out?"

"Good morning. Just went out to get something to eat," he lied. He had been sitting inside the car for a while waiting for Randy's return. He needed to discuss the dream he had last night with him, hoping Randy could help him make up his mind. He still had trouble deciding whether he should save his hooker daughter. The plan that Randy had devised, which required him to be a beggar, was just too humiliating for him to comply. He wished Randy could come up with another plan that would bypass the beggar part.

"Why didn't you come to Stagecoach Inn to have breakfast with us? Those guys kept asking about you."

"Are they still talking about my girl?"

"No more, even Jay Jensen is quiet after I told him don't be a telltale."

"Good. Thank you. I'll come when things quiet down. By the way, do you have a minute? I want to talk to you about a strange dream I had last night."

"What strange dream did you have?"

"Come. I'll make us a fresh pot of coffee."

Randy was amazed when he stepped inside. The drapes were drawn back and windows were wide open, and the house was bright and smelled fresh. No more chaotic messes and vile odors. Everything was in their proper places and the living room was as neat and tidy

33

and clean as he used to seeing it. He must have got over his troubles, Randy thought.

"It isn't Stagecoach Inn coffee, but I hope it is good enough for you." Rob said as he poured Randy and himself a cup.

Randy took a small sip and said, "Not bad, it's almost as good. Now tell me, what kind of strange dream you had last night?"

"You know, Randy, I seldom dream and I never dreamt of my wife before but, last night, very weird, I dreamt of her coming to see me, begging me to save Angie. 'Please save her, Rob, we have only this daughter. I won't have peace if I know her living a terrible life,' she begged me, pulling hard on my sleeve. I wonder if it was a dream at all. It was so real and I can still remember every details. Let me show you the shirt I wore last night, the sleeve is torn at the seam. Mary did it!" Rob went to his room and brought back a shirt to show Randy. Indeed, the left sleeve was torn in such a way that it was evident that it was the result of a violent pull.

"Are you sure? You could have torn it yourself, you know, when you got drunk and a nail may..." Randy knew Rob had been drinking heavily last night because he could smell alcohol and see many yellow stains on his shirt.

"Not a chance! Look at it again, only a forceful pull could have done this!"

Randy picked up the shirt and examined it again, this time very closely. He couldn't find a better explanation for the way it had been torn other than by a nail, it was very obvious to him, but he suddenly came up with a great idea which he thought would make Rob do anything to save his daughter.

"I have to agree with you one hundred percent on this," said Randy seriously, pretending he was absolutely convinced by the evidence. "Mary did it. Remember I've told you that she would be tossing in her grave in agony if you don't try your best to save Angie? It could be her spirit that came to you last night asking for help."

"You really think so? Or are you trying to scare me?"

"I'm not. I've heard so many this kinds of stories and I don't suspect people making them up." Despite Randy said it in a serious tone with straight face, he could barely suppress his outburst of laughter when he saw Rob's frightened face turn white.

Rob was an atheist and an engineer with logical thinking. It was impossible for him to believe the preposterous ghost stories like this. But now his atheistic foundation started to shake and so was his physical self, for he could not explain why he had suddenly dreamt of his deceased wife last night of all nights, why she asked such a favor of all favors and, most strange of all, how to explain the torn sleeve! After taking his time to have another sip of coffee, Rob said reluctantly, "I guess I have to do it then, just to ease my mind. But I still think it's absurd to believe Mary's spirit had paid me a visit last night. It must be the drinking and thinking of her too much lately."

"Whatever it is, I think you should do it," said Randy encouragingly, feeling relieved. For more than a week now, he had been upset with Rob and didn't bother to come to see him. For he thought Rob was wrong; as a responsible father, he should try his very best to save his daughter, no matter how hard, how embarrassing, and how undeserving she was.

"When do you want to start?" asked Randy.

35

"Whenever you're ready, you got to help me on this; I don't have your cleverness. You just tell me what to do and I'll do it."

"Very well, I'll let you know in a few days. Let me do some thinking first. Are you coming tomorrow morning?"

"I better not. I won't feel comfortable seeing those guys yet."

"Up to you, but don't drink and think too much. You don't want to have another bad dream again, do you?"

"Now, don't try to scare me again."

But Rob was afraid that night, afraid of the ghost coming back again in his dream and he felt chilly and eerie. After putting on a sweater and still feeling the same, he went to check the thermometer. It was 78 degree Fahrenheit, which was considered quite warm normally.

"It's warm!" cried he. "I shouldn't feel cold. It must be the heavy drinking lately, which has weakened my body." Rob tried to embolden himself with excuses rather than to admit he was scare.

SEVEN

There was no more ghost visit that night, but that did not mean Rob had slept well. He has been torn between the anticipation of another visit from his ghost wife and the appalling thoughts of acting as a beggar. Even though he had already told Randy that he would do it, he ·actually was not yet ready for it mentally.

Three days later he was still not ready, but Randy was ready. He invited Rob over to have dinner at his house, and after dinner he revealed his new plan which was a lot more agreeable than his last one. It only required Rob to look like a homeless man dressed shabbily and without shaving and bathing for a few days. And, instead of sitting on the sidewalk waiting for people to throw a few coins into his tin can, he would be moving around among people soliciting for changes.

"I like it much better, at least I don't have to sit on the dirty floor and get my ass numbed," laughed Rob.

"I think it'll be more effective, too. By moving around, you'll have a better chance to catch Angie's attention. But be careful not getting too close to her and asking her for changes," Randy teased. He was in much better mood now that Rob was going to follow his plan.

"Of course, do you think I'm stupid?"

"I just worry. Since you're new in the business, you may feel too embarrassed to look at people. You know, I don't want Angie getting suspicious. This is our only chance."

A week later, when Rob's beard and hair were long and untidy enough, he was ready for business. He put on his garden clothes and the pair of old hiking tennis shoes and climbed into Randy's vintage Oldsmobile, going to Lake Eleazy with his heart racing like the car's engine. Because it was still early, there were plenty of empty parking spaces to choose from, Randy parked his car in the one that gave him an unobstructed view of Three Corner, so that he could watch Rob begging, which he thought would be very amusing.

Getting out of the car hesitantly, Rob sauntered down the street towards Three Corner. It was a short walk but it took him a long time to get there, because he had stopped many times, looking backward as if he wasn't sure it was the right thing to do. Every time he passed a shop, he stopped and looked and was startled by what he saw: he did not look like his normal self – a neat and clean engineer wearing long-sleeved white shirt, black dress pants, and polished, brown leather shoes – but did not look like a homeless man either. He just looked like a filthy old man. Nobody would mistake him as a beggar until he opened his mouth asking for money. Even then, people would think he was only a transitory beggar who was forced to beg due to temporary, unfortunate situation. His demeanor was unfit the part he was playing. At first, Rob did his job poorly; he stayed at one place, hanging his head and avoiding eye contacts with people and, when he asked people for money, he asked so hesitantly and inaudibly that nobody took him seriously. But, after getting so many "no" or looking-the-other-way for answers, his facial skin got thicker and he started acting more aggressively; moving freely from place to place and from group to group and, as a result, he put money into his pocket more frequently.

Randy was watching from afar and he was amazed; he did not expect Rob, an inflexible engineer with no business experience, could adapt to panhandling that quickly. But he still had doubt that Rob could control himself should he see his daughter hustling with "johns". Any confrontation between them at this point might jeopardize the rescue mission.

Fortunately, his daughter had not shown up that night and Rob's first night as a panhandler went rather smoothly, even profitably. He emptied his pocket into his worn baseball cap he was wearing and started counting the money the minute he got into Randy's car.

"Wow, not bad, almost thirty bucks for two-and-a-half-hour's work," exclaimed Rob, as excited as a delivery boy when he receives his first tips from an old lady.

"Don't forget, half is mine."

"Half is yours? Did you go out there hustling?"

"No, but I was sitting here in my car the whole time worrying."

Rob understood what Randy meant: he might have lost control of himself should his daughter have appeared. "Thanks God, she didn't come," said Rob cheerfully. "Let's go to have a drink. I buy, with *our* money."

EIGHT

For the next two nights Rob's panhandling still went well except he hadn't seen his daughter yet, which was a sort of relief for him because he was still unprepared to deal with the tense situation should he see her. He was not sure how well he could control his temper, if he could control it at all, under such stressful circumstance. But on the third night something had happened that worried him a lot. He sensed someone had been tailing him, and when he turned around he saw a familiar face that he was quite sure he had seen before, but he couldn't recall when and where. While he was searching his memory bank in frustration, the woman turned around and walked away in a hurry, obviously wanting to avoid him.

When he told Randy about it later, Randy said excitedly, "That's good, very good; someone who knows you saw you and she will tell Angie. The whole purpose of begging near where she works was to let her know, right? Now someone will tell her and she'll appear soon. It can be as soon as tomorrow night."

Rob nodded indifferently, a mixed feeling of anticipation and anxiety had engulfed him momentarily. He wished Randy was wrong and yet, he knew Randy was seldom wrong about things like that.

Near eleven o'clock the next night and it was about time for Rob to go home, he spot the familiar face again. She was among a group of people in front of the drugstore across the street from him, peeking frequently from behind the crowd in his direction and periodically turning around to speak to someone in the group. Rob couldn't see the other person's face but from the body shape he could tell it was a woman. He decided to walk past the group on his way back to Randy's waiting car, to find out whether it was his own imagination or something he had suspected. But, as soon as he crossed the street, the familiar-faced woman, together with the other woman, left the group and went into the drugstore. From the way the other woman walked, Rob was quite sure she was his daughter.

First, Rob had an urge to follow them into the drugstore to find out who they were, but at a second thought he did not think it was a good idea. He was not yet ready to put himself face-to-face with his daughter at this time, in case the other woman was really her. He walked pass the drugstore without looking in and hurried to Randy's car, but before he got in he looked back to make sure no one was following. It did not look right for a beggar to have a ride in a car, even if it was a very old car.

After hearing Rob's close encounter, Randy said, "Great! Very soon you don't have to beg anymore. I bet Angie will call me soon."

"How do you know?"

"If you're sure the other woman is Angie, the one with the familiar face must be Angie's friend who recognizes you—"

"Oh! Now, I remember," Rob cried out elatedly. "She's Angie's schoolmate called Linda. She had come to our house a few times."

"Are you sure?"

"I'm pretty sure. I caught her and Johnny Stewart drinking in my backyard when I came home early one afternoon. You know Johnny Stewart, don't you?"

"Of course, how can I forget him? He was the guy who shouted at me 'what are you gawking at, Old Man?' when I stopped trimming the hedges to watch him coming into your front yard. I was very upset then, because he was so rude and so big-headed. So, I shouted back 'at you, Punk!' as I was shaking my hedge trimmer at him. I'm glad he went away quietly, otherwise, I would have given his hair a good trimming."

They both laughed.

Then, Randy continued, "That explains the whole thing if Linda is Angie's schoolmate. You see, Rob, this Linda saw you begging and she told Angie and brought her out tonight. Apparently, Angie didn't want to meet you and that's why she had avoided you. Now that she has seen you as a beggar herself, she'll call me if she still has any feeling for you. Of course, if she has none she won't call."

"What makes you think she'll call you?"

"Well, if she still loves you, she'll want to help. But she can't do it herself; she needs someone to do it for her. Who's better qualified than me, your old neighbor and friend, for the job?

"She still loves me? Don't make me laugh!"

"You'll see. Give us a few days."

Three days had passed, Angie hadn't called and Randy started to worry. If she has no feeling at all for her father, she wouldn't have gone out that night to watch him beg, he thought. If she still hates him, she wouldn't have avoided him by going into the drugstore. She would've loved to humiliate him in public. Well, perhaps she has trouble deciding what to do; love and hate is a complicated matter. Another day passed, nothing had changed and Randy was getting nervous; his confidence in his own prediction had diminished to the point of disappointment. He just couldn't understand why Angie hadn't call yet; all the logical reasoning told him that she would have. Add to his frustration, Rob came over to mock him, "Has she called yet?"

"Give her more time. She'll call, I can guarantee that." Randy not only consoled his disappointed friend but himself, too.

His consolation did little for Rob whose confidence in his prediction had been plummeting. Rob knew his daughter well and was sure she still hated him. "How can it be possible for a person like her who had said terrible things to her parents, has any feeling?" he said bitterly.

"Let's wait and see," said Randy. That was what he could say at this time. He could only secretly pray Angie wouldn't fail him.

Randy was right, Angie did have trouble deciding what to do with her beggar father. That night after she'd watched her father beg, she had a long discussion with her schoolmate and now roommate, Linda. Linda was only four years older but she was much more mature because she had been through a lot more ups-and-downs of life than Angie. She had been cheated and abused by men so many times that she could hardly trust anybody. But she trusted Angie and treated her like her baby sister. She knew everything about Angie's family because Angie had told her. The night she saw Angie's father panhandling at Three Corner, she was uncertain that he was indeed Angie's father, for she hadn't seen him for a long time and the man she saw was old and shabby, in total contrast to the neat and clean engineer she remembered. She called Angie on her smart phone right away and urged her to come to take a look, but Angie was tied up with a customer at the time and couldn't come. But next night they came together and saw the beggar whom Angie confirmed was indeed her father. But she couldn't muster the nerve to face him because of so many reasons that she didn't even know what they exactly were, except this one: she was afraid of him. She was afraid he might scold and embarrass her in front of people in this small community where she lived and worked.

"What the hell you're doing, trying to numb yourself by drinking?" asked Linda when she saw Angie drinking tequila directly from the bottle.

"What else can I do!" said Angie angrily. "Why can't he leave me alone? Now that he's begging in my territory, pretty soon the whole fucking town will know that my Daddy is a beggar. How the hell can I continue to stay here if I can't hold up my Goddamn head?"

"Well, what are you going to do about it?"

"Damn it! I don't know, I just don't know!" exclaimed Angie in frustration. "I may have to hire a Goddamn thug to chase him out of this shitty place or to kill him if necessary."

"Strange, very strange!" muttered Linda, deep in thought.

"What's so Goddamn strange? Angie asked, awfully annoyed.

"You know what," said Linda, "your father has a house and I'm sure he also has savings and pensions, something like that. Why has he become a beggar and chosen to beg in this lousy town, of all the towns in the world?"

"Yes! Why? Why he must do it in this Goddamn town! He could've chosen Tamekola, Marietta, or Moon City. Any of these towns is richer than ours here. Some Goddamn people who know my father and me must have told him I work here. Have you told him, Linda?"

"Are you accusing me, Angie? Would I do a thing like that? No, I have not! As a matter of fact, I haven't seen him ever since that day about five years ago when he caught Johnny and I drinking in your backyard. Boy! Was he mean! He chased us off with a shotgun that scared the shit out of us."

"I wish he'd blown you two stupid heads off."

"Why?"

"Why! You know who paid for what you two crazy, stupid juveniles did? Me, your poor Angie! That night, he chewed me up like you chew your Goddamn chewing gum, for hours."

"I'm sorry. It was Johnny's idea, not mine, and we didn't expect your father come home so early."

"It's all right. Now, tell me truthfully why my Daddy has become a beggar and why you told him to beg here?"

"Damn it, Angie! How many times I have to tell you that I haven't told your father anything!" Linda was mad. She hated people falsely accused her for something she hadn't done. She was a forthright sort of a person but she had a hot temper.

"If not you, who the hell could've done it, you're the only person who knows my Daddy and also knows about me."

"C'mon, you know there are a lot of people who know your father, any one of them might have told him. Angie, you must find out, it is very puzzling."

"But how, go to ask my father myself? I can't do that, can I? I'd promised myself never to speak to him again. By the way, I don't give a shit who the Goddamn informant is and why my Daddy has become a beggar as long as he isn't begging in where I make my living. It makes me sick to see him begging. Oh, Linda, can you do me a big favor?"

"What?"

"Next time when you see him tell him not to bother me anymore, will you? Tell him to go somewhere else to beg, any Goddamn place if I care!"

"How can I do that, he has the right to beg where the hell he wishes, unless we send him away with some money."

"Give him some money, then! Ask him how much he wants and I'll give you the Goddamn dough. Just help me to get rid of him, ok?"

"Ok," answered Linda apathetically. She thought Angie was wrong; she shouldn't have treated her father just like another beggar. She should try to help him. But Linda knew it was no use at this time to reason with Angie; she was just too full of hatred to be reasoned. This was not the first time Linda thought Angie was wrong. The first time was when Angie ran away from home. Linda had tried but in vain to persuade her going home by exaggerating the horror and danger that a runaway would have to face. She always envied Angie had such caring and loving parents that she never had and wished to have. She never understood why Angie was willing to forgo a loving home where she was treated like a princess to become a hooker who was scorned and abused. But Linda should have known, Angie has been spoiled and she had drug problem.

NINE

Cannot resist Angie's repeated pleadings, Linda went to Three Corner earlier than usual the following night; she wanted to talk to Angie's father before the place was getting too busy, for she might have to go out with a customer later. She didn't have to wait very long before she saw him coming out of the back alley, wearing the same outfit as the night before and holding a walking stake in one hand and a tin cup in the other. She followed him for a while and when she got close enough to him she called softly from behind: "Mr. Taylor, wait, I need to talk to you."

Rob stopped and turned around. "Yes, you are—do I know you?"

"I'm Linda, Angie's schoolmate, remember me?

"Oh, yes, I caught you and John Stewart drinking in our backyard."

"It was a long time ago," said Linda, embarrassed. "May I have a word with you, Mr. Taylor?" Getting no objection Linda continued, "Follow me, please." She led him to the small beach on the other side of Lakeside Drive. It was still early, only a few underprivileged teen-agers were there playing Frisbees. Drug addicts and drug pushers had not arrived yet.

"What do you want to talk to me about, Linda?" asked Rob uncertainly. He did not expect his daughter would send someone instead of coming to talk to him her-self.

"Angie sent me to ask you a few questions."

"Go ahead," said Rob calmly. But inside him he felt extremely edgy. What's it that she wants to know and why she doesn't come to ask me herself? He asked all these questions in his head, very much baffled.

"She wants to know why you have to beg and why you choose here to beg." Linda said bluntly, she was not a sophisticate person and she didn't know how to present it tactfully.

"Tell her, it's none of her business."

"It is. She wants to give you some money so that you don't have to beg," said Linda timidly.

"Why is she so generous and kind all of a sudden, her conscience is bothering her?" Despite his remark was full of mockery, Rob was pleased to know that his daughter still care about him. Randy is right, he thought.

"No, not her conscience, it is your begging that bothers her. You see, Mr. Taylor, Angie has a lot of friends here; if they know her father is a beggar, they'll look her down and she won't be able to hold up her head."

"Who does she think she is, the Law, tells me what I can and cannot do? What I do and where I want to do it is none of her business, tell her that! Also, tell her do not worry about me competing with her for business, I'm a beggar not a hooker and at least I don't have to sell my body." Rob was furious. Such a cold, business-like and unfeeling request was not what he had expected from his daughter. Now, Rob understood the true motive of his daughter's generosity – not out of kind and love as he had first thought but out of the fear that his presence might have brought her shame. "How can a beggar father bring more shame to an already very shameful hooker daughter?" asked Rob, followed by an outburst of uncontrollable laughter, a rather angry and scornful laughter.

Suddenly, Linda saw the same angry, hollering Mr. Taylor of years ago when she was caught drinking in his backyard. She was frightened and trembling then, so was
48

she now. Mr. Taylor's rather absurd laughter had made her mighty uncomfortable, and she didn't know what to do but to pray it would stop. Only then, she stuttered, "Look, Mr. Taylor, please understand Angie and I just want to help."

"Help, from you?" Rob burst out another sarcastic laughter. "What makes you think I need help from your kind? She's no daughter of mine and I hardly know you." Rob got really upset now and started walking away. He took the offer from the girls as an insult.

"Wait, Mr. Taylor, Angie wants to know how much you want not to beg any more in this area. You know, she lives and works here…" Linda's words were like oil on fire, they only made Rob angrier. He walked away without turning or answering, but cussing a thousand times in his head.

Linda looked embarrassed. She felt sick in the stomach for failing her mission and, instead, getting an insult from a beggar. And she knew why. She had related Angie's message too bluntly, which gave Rob Taylor an impression that his daughter found his panhandling in Lake Eleazy a nuisance and wanted to get rid of him with a bribe. "Why I'm so dumb said such horrible things, even I, myself, don't like to hear that!" she blamed herself out loud afterward.

But Linda told Angie a different story when she reported back to her later that night; she did not want to hurt her by telling her the truth. She just told her that her father refused to speak to her no matter how hard she'd tried. .She suggested Angie to enlist someone who knows her father well to help.

"Oh, Uncle Randy!" cried Angie excitedly. "If anyone knows anything about my Daddy, Uncle Randy should know. He's our next-door neighbor and my Daddy's best friend. Shit, I don't have his number anymore."

"You can go to talk to him."

"No! I can't go back there; everybody will recognize me."

"I'll go for you if you want me to."

"Will you? Great! Do you still remember our house?"

"I think so. Is his house on the left of your father's?'

"No, on the right, he has a fountain in his front yard. When can you go?"

"I can go after breakfast, tomorrow."

"Not so early though. He always has breakfast at Stagecoach Inn."

"I won't. Shit, I forgot! Our breakfast is other people's lunch. Do you think he'll be home in the afternoon?"

"He should," said Angie who was very happy and drunk now that she fell into sleep right on the couch.

Lately, Randy had been staying home a lot more than usual. The only time he was out was going to Stagecoach Inn to have breakfast and a trip to a neighborhood grocery store. He carried the wireless phone with him wherever he went around the house and was waiting anxiously for Angie to call. But Angie *didn't* call. Though getting frustrated after many days of disappointment, he hadn't lost hope; in fact, his hope was getting more robust after Rob had told him his encounter with Linda.

"I was right and I was wrong," said Randy, laughing aloud. "I was right that Angie still cares about her father, and I was wrong that her concern is not his wellbeing but his meddling of her business. I didn't expect she still hates her father that much after all these years; time had done nothing to soft her heart. How could a nice little girl turn into such…?"

While he was mulling over his predictions and reasoning, he heard a few soft knocks at the door and he shouted, "Come in, it's open," thinking it was either Rob or the gardener who came for his monthly maintenance fees.

"It's locked." He heard a woman's voice which he thought was Angie's.

"I'm sorry, I thought it's open," he apologized as he walked quickly to the door. "What can I do for you, Miss?" asked Randy, rather disappointed. The woman standing in front of him was not Angie but a total stranger.

"Are you Mr. Gibbs?"

"Yes, I'm."

"My name is Linda, Angie Taylor's friend. She sent me here to talk to you."

"Of course, come on in," said Randy in a very friendly voice. He was ecstatic that his prediction finally proved to be right.

After Randy had Linda seated and handed her a glass of ice water, he asked casually, "How's Angie? Is she okay? Why didn't she come to see me herself?"

"She's fine, just fine. She can't come because she said she's afraid…She wants to call you but she doesn't have your number."

"I understand. Now, tell me what she wants to talk to me about."

"She wants to find out a few things about her father and she needs your help." Linda was careful with her wording this time; she had learned her lesson well: she must not speak to old gentlemen like Rob and Randy the same way as she normally did to younger people living in her Lake Eleazy neighborhood.

"What does she want to know?"

"She wants to know why her father has become a beggar.

"He is broke. When you're broke and have nobody supporting you, what would you do?"

"He isn't poor, is he? He had a good job before and owns a house. By the way, is he still living next door?"

"Yes, he still lives next door but he doesn't own it anymore, I do. I bought it from him and let him live in it so he won't be a homeless man. Ever since his daughter ran away and his wife committed suicide, Mr. Taylor had been drinking heavily, day and night, and blowing his money on gambling. You know, he seldom got drunk before except on a few special occasions, and he never smoked or gambled. I guess he wanted to kill himself just like his wife did. All these are the paybacks from his darling daughter. She has broken her parents' hearts and destroyed a good family. What a sad story, I just don't understand how a lovely girl like her could do a thing like that." Randy intentionally exaggerated his accounts of Rob in order to paint a dire picture of him to touch Angie's conscience – to make her feel guilty and responsible for her father's demise.

Linda was wordless but her heart was warmed by what she had just heard; all her life she had been neglected, abused, and mistreated – in broken home with an uncaring mother and two abusive stepfathers and later in the mean streets of Lake Eleazy – she never knew what friendship and love was. She couldn't believe there was a person in this world so generous and compassionate in helping a friend, while Angie was only interested in getting rid of her own father. All of a sudden, she had great respect for this stranger she met for the first time, greater than she ever had for anybody else. But, she still did not understand why Randy blamed her friend, Angie, for her parents' problems. That's not fair! She thought. Angie hasn't done anything to cause her father's downfall which was his own doing. Nobody forced him to drink and to gamble. Since Angie was not present to defend herself, she decided to do it for her as a good friend should. "May I ask why you blame all these on Angie, Mr. Gibbs? I don't see she's done anything wrong." asked Linda, trying hard to present her question politely, though she thought Randy's criticism of her friend was too harsh and unfair.

"I'll tell you why, young lady. She ran away from home," said Randy authoritatively, like a strict father to his children.

"It's not a crime to run away from home," said Linda defiantly. The mere mentioning of "run away from home" had brought back all those painful memories which made her sad and angry. "I've done it myself. If you were me, beaten and sexually abused by your stepfather, you would have done the same thing. Believe me; to survive out there in the streets alone is not easy, it is downright miserable and dangerous. But it's much better than staying home and letting my stepfather..." Recalling all the awful things her stepfather had done to her, Linda started to sob.

This time it was Randy's turn to be wordless; he had never thought of that there are good children driven out of homes by bad parents. He always thought all the runaways are bad children. He was moved, feeling awfully sorry for the girl whom he considered, only a minute ago, a no-good person.

Handing her a tissue, Randy said gently, "I'm sorry, Linda, I'm really sorry for you to have such a lousy family. But Angie's case is different; she has wonderful parents who love her very much, treating her like a princess. It was Angie, who took it for granted, hanging out with the wrong kind of people, getting into alcohol and drugs and finally into dirty movie business. She caused the death of her mother by breaking her heart, caused her father to lose interest to live, spending all his money on gambling and getting drunk every day. Are these not enough?"

There was nothing for Linda to say. What Randy had just told her was new to her, Angie never told her this; she only told her how mean her parents were – how she had been slapped on the face by her hysterical mother and kicked out of the house and her mother's funeral by her quick-tempered father. And Linda believed her because she had had first-handed bad experiences with her stepfathers. Now, she felt deceived and was angry at Angie. "I'm really sorry to hear this," said Linda after a long pause. "I didn't know. I thought I can help Angie to reconcile with her father so that she can go home and have a good life again. She's still young, you know. Well, I guess nothing I can do now. Thank you for telling me this. Well, I better get going." Linda got up and about to leave.

"Wait, may I ask you a question?"

"Sure, Mr. Gibbs," said Linda, sitting down again.

"Do you really want to help Angie?"

"Yes, I did, but not anymore."

"Tell me why you wanted to help her."

"Well—well," Linda stuttered, feeling uncomfortable with the question. "You see, Mr. Gibbs, I don't have a nice family. My mother married three times and all my stepfathers and their children treated me badly, like I was an outcast, so I ran away when I was old enough. When Angie ran away from home, I felt it was my fault because I thought I was a bad influence for her. I introduced her to bad people and a bad lifestyle. But I love Angie, she's a good girl and very smart. She shouldn't be in the business

54

we're in. I urge her to quit and find a better life, but, you know, it isn't easy to get out once you're knee-deep in it."

"Why don't you quit yourself?" asked Randy suspiciously. He liked what Linda had said so far but he doubted that it was from her heart. Randy was an ultra-conservative; he still believed in people-profiling. He never regarded highly of prostitutes.

"Well, Mr. Gibbs, I've been in the business too long and am not smart like Angie. I don't know anything else to make a living. Besides, I'm too old to hope for a better future. I have to accept that my life is done."

"You're not. Please stay for a little while. I have a plan to get you both out if you care to hear. Now, let me make us a pot of fresh coffee." Randy was absolutely touched by Linda's honest assessment of herself and he felt sorry for her. She seems to be a good girl, why not save her, too, he thought.

Neither of them said anything as Linda watched Randy meticulously brewing coffee. Linda was wondering what Randy meant by "I have a plan to get you both out". At the same time, Randy was pondering how to approach Linda so that she could be of help in getting Angie out of the fire pit.

Finally, Randy spoke after he had put a cup of coffee in front of Linda. "Linda, I believe what you've just told me is all true and I apologize for what I've told you aren't entirely true. Almost all true except the part that Angie's father has gambled away all his money and I've bought his house. You see, I'm like you, want to help a friend. Ever since Angie left home and her mother committed suicide because of Angie—"

"Angie didn't tell me her mother had committed suicide. She said her mother died because her father had been mistreating her."

"No, that's not true. Angie had killed her mother, at least indirectly. She died of heartbreak. You see, Angie is their only child, their princess and they loved her very much, may be too much in my opinion. Angie's parents are nice people; they never raise their voices at each other, I know because we are neighbors. Her runaway changed everything. They constantly argued and fought and her father began drinking heavily. His drinking got worse after his wife died, making his house look and smell like a trash dump. He wanted to kill himself, I guess, because Angie had hurt him so bad that he had no desire to live. As a friend and neighbor I want to help, but the only way I can help him, I figure, is to help him get his princess back. I know he still loves Angie; parents never stop loving their children no matter how much they had hurt them. So, I came up with this idea of making him a beggar begging at Three Corner in Lake Eleazy—"

"You're a very kind man, Mr. Gibbs," Linda cut in. Now that Randy had given her the answers that she and Angie wanted to know, she was obligated to return the favor by opening up herself to him. "But I doubt your plan will work because Angie is a very stubborn girl and she still hates her father very much."

"It will, with your help," said Randy confidently as he reached for the pot of coffee to refill Linda's cup and his.

"Me, you need my help?" Linda was amazed; she couldn't believe that she could be of any help in a complicated situation like this. A wise gentleman like you needs help from an ignorant girl like me? You must be kidding, she thought.

"Yes, my dear, we need your help. Without your help, I doubt we can succeed."

"How can I help you?" Linda got excited by Randy's flattery, for the first time in her life she felt useful and important.

Instead of answering her question, Randy picked up the phone to call Rob Taylor. "Rob, can you come over, I want you to meet a person."

Rob and Linda were both startled to see each other; Rob did not expect to see her here in Randy's house and he suspected what was the reason, and Linda was in awe when she saw the transformation of the beggar she met only a day before. He was totally a different man now, wearing a white cotton long-sleeved shirt and a pair of light brown khakis and despite he still had a beard and long hairs, they were clean and well-kept. He was a very respectable-looking man indeed.

"Let me introduce to you, Rob, this is Linda. Linda, this is Rob—"

"We have met," they both said.

"Oh, I didn't know, but great! Do you care for a cup of coffee, Rob, before we start?"

"No, thank you, I just had some."

"Linda, do you mind telling Mr. Taylor what you've just told me. I think Mr. Taylor wants to hear it himself, oh, the whole thing, please."

Dutifully Linda repeated her story and when she finished she looked at Rob anxiously, expecting to find signs of gratitude from his expression. But there was no such a sign; he only said apathetically: "I can't believe a person like her has a friend like you."

Linda was confused; she did not know what Rob meant by this. As a veteran hooker and had exposed herself to many different kinds of people, she knew it was a double talk, which could mean either good or bad.

But Randy was not confused; he knew precisely what Rob meant, for he knew him for a long time and knew him well. Rob was an engineer whose profession required him to be exact and thus made him inflexible. He had low opinion of other professions, much less for dubious professions like prostitution and adult movie industry.

"I've explained to Linda our plan, Rob, and she agrees to help. She's a good girl and has contemplated to quit that lousy business for a long time and she wants Angie to quit, too. With her help, our chance of success will be much greater."

"If Linda can help, that will be great. Can I stop begging yet?"

"Not yet, not until Angie and I have a meeting first. Oh, Linda, you must not tell Angie about our conversations—also don't tell her you've met her Daddy. You go back there and tell her that I was very upset that she didn't come to see me herself. You give her my number and tell her to call me if she wants my help. You don't need to do anything, just leave everything to me."

"That's all?"

"Yes, that's all. Oh, there is one more thing you may do: lie to Angie that I am a gentleman and am very nice to you."

"It's true, I don't have to lie!" said Linda innocently, not knowing Randy was joking.

TEN

Back to their apartment in Lake Eleazy, Linda followed Randy's order strictly; she didn't tell Angie much, except saying Uncle Randy was very upset with her when she gave her the piece of paper containing his phone number. She didn't tell her Randy's plan to save her and the meeting with her father.

"That's all?" Angie asked skeptically. "You've been gone for three hours."

"Your Uncle Randy is not a friendly guy. He didn't even let me in at first."

"Why you stayed there that long then?"

"I did not. I went to the Mall looking around. You know whom I bumped into, Angie?"

"Who"

"Kathy Simpson. She told me she'd got married and had two kids now, a boy and a girl. She looks great and very—."

"Never mind that bitch," Angie interjected. What about my Daddy? You didn't see him?"

"Yes," Linda's tongue had slipped, but she corrected herself quickly with a "No."

"Damn it, can't you give me a straight answer? You got me all freaking confused."

"I said: 'Yes, I didn't see your father.' Or 'No, I didn't see your father.' Did I make myself clear?" Linda pretended to be annoyed by Angie's stupidity and thus covered her own mistakes quickly. "Oh! I'd better go out to get something to eat, I'm starving. Do you want something?"

"No. Thanks."

"Don't forget to call your Uncle Randy. He said you can call him if you need his help."

As soon as Linda went out, Angie called Randy. She did not want Linda to listen to their conversation which she expected to be a very difficult one.

"Uncle Randy, it's me, Angie. How're you?"

"I'm fine. How about you? What have you been doing all these years?" Randy knew what Angie had been doing; he just wanted to give her a hard time. He loved her and wanted to save her, but he was angry at her for what she did for a living.

"I'm all right, just surviving."

"Just surviving," Randy murmured. "A gal called Linda came to see me this afternoon, she said you sent her. Why didn't you come yourself? What do you want of me?" Randy pretended incensed.

"I'm really sorry, Uncle Randy, I don't have your phone number and I'm afraid to come, you know what I mean. Can we meet some place? I need to talk to you."

"We haven't talked for years, what have we to talk about now?" said Randy, still pretending upset. But, when he sensed the other party was also uptight, he worried his pretense might have gone a little too far. In order to keep Angie from hanging up, he added in a cooler tone: "We can talk now on the phone."

"It's not convenient, Uncle Randy, and I need your help. Please give me a chance, meet me some place. How about we meet halfway at Barony's in Marietta? It is on Cal Oak by the freeway, across the street from the gas station."

"It's fine."

"How about in half an hour?" asked Angie, excitement in her voice.

The meeting was cordial and went smoothly – they talked mostly about things in general and tried hard not getting into personal stuffs until later on when they were talking about Angie's runaway, then, she got emotional and raised her voice.

"Calm down, don't talk so loud. Maybe we should find another place to talk." said Randy, feeling awfully uncomfortable when he saw heads turning and eyes gawking in their direction. Even their server acted strangely when she came over to take their orders. Who wouldn't give them a long, suspicious look? He regretted he didn't foresee the problem, otherwise, he would've told Angie to dress more conservatively to the meeting. A half-naked, sexy woman was just too much not to attract unnecessary attentions at a family restaurant.

"Let's talk in my car," suggested Randy once they were outside in the parking lot. "We can talk more freely."

They drove to a neighborhood park nearby and parked at an isolated corner where they could talk with the windows down and without having to worry about other people eavesdropping.

"Now, tell me how I can help," asked Randy as soon as he turned off the engine.

"Can you talk to my Daddy not to beg in Lake Eleazy?"

"Why, because he makes you look bad for having a beggar father?" Randy was irritated by Angie's request; she was more concerned about herself than her father's well-being. She should've asked why her father had become a beggar and how she could help.

"Yes, Uncle Randy, I got a lot of friends there. If they know my father is a beggar, they'll look down on me. You see, it'll ruin my livelihood. I'm willing to give him money every month so he doesn't have to beg."

"You got a lot of friends?" jeered Randy. "My dear Angie, the only friend you got is Linda, and nobody can look you down any more because you have been down for a long time and can't go any lower. My dear, you've really disappointed me; you don't give a damn about your own father! You know why he's a beggar? It's because of you!" Randy lost his usual cool and forgot his mission momentarily, Angie's selfishness and lack of sympathy for her father had really infuriated him. His normally healthy-looking face turned dark and his normally soft and soothing voice became sharp and punishing.

"I always thought you and Aunt Edith were nice people, but I was wrong. You're no different from my parents; you all blame me for everything. Tell me, what have I done to cause Daddy becoming a beggar, uh?" Angie was mad and became confrontational; she had also forgotten at whom she was yelling.

"A lot," Randy said forcefully. "You shouldn't have hung around with those bad kids to do drugs and alcohol. You should have spent more time on your study like Amy Lee and Susan Rodriquez. They are immigrant children, not born in this country and they couldn't speak English when they came, and their parents were not as rich as yours. Look at them now, they're all college graduates and have good paying jobs. And you, hanging around at street corners waiting for immoral people to pick you up and use your body as a relief valve. You should've known better that your bad behavior and defiant attitude had hurt your parents so much that your mother killed herself..."

Randy had accidentally touched Angie's hot-button – her sore and most sensitive spot.

"Damn it! Stop it! I don't have to take your shit!" Angie shouted. "What's so great about Amy Lee and Susan Rodriquez? What's the big deal about their lousy jobs and college degrees? I make more money in an hour than they make in a week!" Angie was in a rage and out of control, she had forgotten she was talking to her elder and using vulgar language was extremely improper. It was no denial that she detested people comparing her with other good neighborhood girls, it was painful to be reminded of her own failure; but nothing she hated more was the reminder of her mother's death was her fault, because the pain brought by the thought that she had killed her mother was torturous and unbearable. She tried to open the car door to get out but her left arm was caught by Randy's firm hand.

"Listen, you let me finish!" ordered Randy, his right hand was still holding on her arm and tried to pull her back. "This probably will be the last time I ever speak to you."

"You're hurting my arm, Uncle Randy!" The pain in her arm and Randy's stern voice had brought her back from her madness. She now realized the man she was talking to was not one of her own kind but an old neighbor whom she called Uncle Randy.

"I'm sorry," said Randy as he let go her arm quickly. "Please listen to me, your parents love you very much and I love you, too. Do you understand?"

"Nobody asked them to love me!" retorted Angie.

"Yes, nobody asked them to love you and they don't have to. They loved you on their own freewill and they couldn't help it. You were so beautiful a child, so cute that it was impossible not to love you; even they knew it might have spoiled you. If you were ours, Edith and I would have done exactly the same thing."

Judging from the way Angie was sitting silently in the car and making no more attempts to leave, Randy knew his adulatory strategy had worked well on her, even though she still had her head turning away from him and gazing outside the window. So he threw at her some more: "You know, I always thought you are the smartest girl among all our neighbors' kids. If you hadn't gone astray, your accomplishment would have far exceeded theirs."

"Can I leave now, Uncle Randy? I really have enough lectures from you," said Angie coolly. She was annoyed by Randy's compliments which she construed as mockeries.

"Angie, Angie, please cool down," said Randy soothingly, he had to be careful with this hothead sitting beside him for she might walk out on him anytime. "Edith and I loved you very much; we'd considered you as our own daughter. Believe me; I have no reason to lie to you. If you care to listen, which you should if you still love your parents. I'll tell you everything after you left home. Want to hear?" Angie remained seated for a nod. The words "if you still love your parents" had pinned her down. If she left now, that meant she did not love her parents, but she still *did*, deep down and perhaps without knowing it herself, although she always spoke the opposite.

"After you left," Randy began, "your parents argued a lot; they blamed each other for your running away. Your Mom cried all the time and your Daddy started smoking and drinking like a fish. I've tried to reason them but they told me they'd lost the purpose to live. Do you understand what they meant, Angie? They had no desire to live without you. Well, your Mom died within a year and your Daddy was devastated. He drank more and more and was drunk all the time, day and night, and also had stopped

64

going to Stagecoach Inn in the morning. You should have seen *your* house, it was a mess; empty liquor bottles and cigarette butts and dirty cups and plates were all over the place. It looked like a trash dump and smelt like one, too. Only after I'd come over every day for more than a week to bring him foods and help him cleaning up the mess that he'd finally quitted doing those foolish things."

At that point, though Angie was still turning her back to Randy and looking out the window, her lips was trembling, trying hard to suppress a good cry, but she couldn't suppress the tears from streaming down her cheeks. Randy's narrative of her parents' reactions to her runaway was so powerful that it reached down to the deepest part of her heart, bringing up the love that had been locked up for years to the surface. Yet, the hatred for her parents, especially for her father, was too strong and persistent – the pain from the slap by her mother, the humiliating shouts of her father to order her out of the house, and the embarrassing expulsion from her mother's funeral service were still loud and clear – that she couldn't replace it with love.

"But, after hearing somebody had seen you peddling yourself at Three Corner," continued Randy, "he locked himself at home for days – drinking, smoking, and not eating – doing the same foolish things again just like before. It took me three days to make him finally open the door for me. 'Please don't try, Randy, let me die. I'd killed my daughter and my wife, and now, I want to kill myself so that I can join them and make up to them.' That was what he said to me. And I said, 'you can't die, Rob, your daughter is still alive. You must save her if you still love her.' Then, he said, 'How can I save her, she died long time ago, besides, I'm a lousy father and a lousy husband and I'm not fit to be either one.' By then, I knew your Daddy still loves you very much and will forgive you for all your wrongs. The only way I could think of to convince him to give up killing himself was to help him to save you, to get you back. So, I proposed to him a plan to save you, which was to persuade him to become a beggar and to beg where you work. You know how hard it is for him to be a beggar and go begging? He wouldn't have done it for a million dollars, but he did it for you because he loves you. He still loves you, Angie!"

The emotional gate of Angie's was broken like a dam by a very powerful earthquake; she jerked away from the window and flung herself into Uncle Randy's arms, burying her face on his chest and crying like a baby. She was overcome by shame and remorse. Randy's every word was like a lightning rod, which had cracked open the door of her conscience. She regretted being so thoughtless and selfish, saying such heartless things. "I do give a damn about Daddy. Why can't I say it? Why I'm so proud and stubborn to admit it?" she inwardly screamed at herself.

Randy, feeling the wetness on his chest, laid his hand on Angie's head and caressed her hair and said comfortingly, "Don't cry, be brave. Everything will be all right!"

With tears still in her eyes, Angie raised her head and looked at Randy and said, "I'm terribly sorry, Uncle Randy, I shouldn't have said what I'd said. I don't know why I hate Daddy so much and can't admit I do care about him. Now, what do you want me to do?"

"We want you to move back home and we'll help you to find something nice to do."

"Let me think about it first," That was all Angie had to say before they parted.

ELEVEN

Angie had been thinking about it for days now and thinking hard, too, but she still couldn't make up her mind. It was one of the most difficult decisions she ever had to make. It involved a drastic change of friends, of environment and lifestyle, and more importantly, she wasn't sure she could survive without drugs. Moving back home guaranteed there would be none. Furthermore, she had no confidence that she and her father could get along; she still hated him when ugly old memories resurfaced. Emotion was still high and intense when she recalled what had happened the night she ran away and how he had chased her out of the funeral parlor in front of so many people when she wanted to pay her mother a last respect. And as to her career, what could she do? She had no college degree and no other skills besides the one she had now to earn a decent living. Could she be happy with minimum wage and working long hours like a donkey? "Well, if I don't do what Uncle Randy asked me to do," Angie talked to herself aloud, "what will happen to Daddy? Do I want to kill him like I did to Mom? Oh, what a deep shit I'm in, I'd better talk it over with Linda tonight. That little cunning bitch may have some good ideas."

That night, before they left their apartment to hustle at Three Corner, Angie made a pitcher of margarita and invited Linda to have a drink with her.

"Isn't it too early for that," asked Linda, baffled. "What's the occasion?"

"Nothing in particular, come, sit down here. I need to talk to you."

"Can't we wait until after work? It's getting late and I have to get ready."

"Let's take a night off. We can go down to Tamekola to watch a movie or something afterward. We need to relax once in a while, don't we? All work and no play make us a dull girl."

"I don't think Cowboy would like it very much, he'll come to have our asses kicked. We're already a week behind on our dues, remember? Are you not afraid he'll cut off your supply?"

"C'mon, let's not worry about these shits tonight; I got something very, very important to discuss with you. Ok?"

"What?" Linda faked her ignorance. She knew what it was all about and she had been anxiously waiting for this moment for days.

"You know I went to see Uncle Randy, don't you?

"No. You didn't tell me."

"Do you know what he wants from me? To go home and find a decent job!"

"That's great!

"Damn it, be serious! What do you mean, great?

"Why not? We'll have a real home, won't have to pay for the rent and the Goddamn protection dues, and won't have to stand at street corners waiting..."

"That's enough! What do you mean "we"? Are you invited to move in with my Daddy, too?"

"I'm sure it'll be all right with him. If he doesn't want me, Uncle Randy might."

"Ok, suppose we both can move back home, what can we do, be a dishwasher ruining our nails by washing dirty dishes all night or be a poor waitress letting some dirty old men pinch our cheeks? We got no skills, Linda, and the jobs we can handle pay very little, not even enough to pay for the food. Where are we going to get the dough for booze and dope and new clothes?"

"We can do without them; at least we have a future. What we're doing now has no future. Yes, we make quite a bit more money, but we have to pay those fucking bastards protection money, buy booze and drugs to numb ourselves, and after all these we have nothing left to be saved for the future. Open your eyes and look around us, Angie, how many sisters we know had saved enough to afford a decent retirement? None! The clever and lucky ones end up as mamas, managing a horde of little bitching chickens, but they have to kiss everybody's ass, including ours. Not an easy job, Angie. For those who can't find asses to kiss, they're still working in the streets at retirement age and getting only ten bucks a shot if they are lucky. And don't forget, Angie, we're getting what we ask for now because we're still young and attractive, but as we get older, our prices will go lower very quickly. Shit, I almost forgot, the thing I hate most is to let those filthy and stinking bastards climb on top of me and doing the meanest thing imaginable. Remember the jerk who'd hurt you so badly with a spiky thing that you had been bleeding and crying for days? It made me sick to see you get tortured and humiliated like that."

"Damn you, don't ever bring that up again! It makes me freaking sick to my stomach!"

"I'm terribly sorry," said Linda as she leaned over to touch Angie's hand. Suddenly, she shouted elatedly, "Why, I have an idea. We can quit this lousy business and still can make tons of dough."

"How? It's only eight o'clock in the evening, too early to dream, Linda!"

"But this time, I can assure you, my dream will come true. You'll see."

"Oh yeah, tell me why it's different this time," asked Angie. She was somewhat excited by the confident look on Linda's face. It was true that most of Linda's dreams remained dreams, but once in a blue moon they became realities. Being an old friend of Linda, she knew her well. Linda was quite a character; she was naïve and impractical, unscrupulous and immoral, and a cunning manipulator who had a knack for taking advantage of people or situations. But, she wasn't all bad; she was daring and street smart and extremely loyal and honest to her few friends, of which Angie by far her most favorite.

"You know what, Angie; I have this idea for days now and I haven't got the time to tell you. You know every trade has a union, right?"

"So?"

"But there is no union for our trade. Why can't we start one? We can unionize our sisters, helping them to get rid of those fucking, blood-sucking pimps, to bargain for a better working condition, to set up pension plans for them and, oh yes, to have stricter rules for "johns" so they'll have to behave like school boys. And even better yet, we'll require our client to make an appointment first, just like the doctor's office, so that our sisters don't have to stand at street corners anymore. Just to imagine, Angie, we'll be sitting in our office counting the money rolling in…"

"Save your breath, Linda, it won't work," said Angie after she let Linda finish her dream.

"Why not? You always pour ice water on my fire!"

"I try to be honest with you. Do you really think those fucking pimps like Cowboy will let us form a union and get rid of them without a fight? How can we fight those mean bastards? Use your stupid head, Linda!"

"No sweat! We can hire the mafia to help us, just like other unions do."

"Don't be stupid; it is like introducing wolves to kill the coyotes."

Linda gave up arguing, she could never win when she argued with Angie whom she thought was smarter because Angie had finished high school while she went to grade school only. She went back to surf the internet and Angie went back to her pitcher of margarita, thinking how ludicrous Linda's idea was. All of a sudden, Linda screamed again, even more elatedly, "Angie, pour me another one," she pointed at the pitcher of margarita. "This one must work!"

"What's it?" asked Angie as she refilled Linda's glass. Linda's enthusiasm had never failed to energize her.

"Ok, we quit the street hooker business and go into internet hooker business."

"What! You must be out of your Goddamn mind, Linda; we don't know a fucking thing about computer…"

"We know how to use a smart phone, do we?"

"So?"

"We set up a website and put some nude pictures of ourselves in it. When those sex maniacs call our cells, we'll show them what they want to see and talk to them what they want to hear."

"Through the phone and we don't have to let them climb on top of us? Great! I like that. But how can we get their dough?"

"My dear Angie, how naïve you are; you don't know we can charge their credit cards?"

"No, I don't. How can we get hold of their credit cards if we aren't with them? Ask them to FedEx us?"

"You're so ignorant, Angie. There're companies that can provide the service for a fee. Never mind, I think it's too complicated for you to understand. You just answer the phone and make them stay on the phone as long as possible because we charge them by the time they're on the phone with you. And I'll handle the business end of it, understand?"

"Why I have to answer the Goddamn phone? What about you, just sitting on your fat ass collecting money like a pimp?"

"You're so Goddamn dumb, Angie. You see, you're younger and prettier and have a better-looking body than mine, so you're more marketable. You can make those fucking freaks want to see more and talk longer. Don't you understand? I believe you should take a couple of marketing classes at Moon City Community College."

"Perhaps I should, so that I can make you answer the Goddamn phone." Angie was not very happy being called dumb by someone whom she considered illiterate and stupid.

"All right, let's not argue at this point. Perhaps, we both have to answer the phone at the beginning before we've made enough money to hire some younger girls to do it. But, for now our only problem is that we have no money to set up a website. I figure we have to play along with your Uncle Randy's proposal: you move back home and I move in with him. And then we have to figure out a way to get the money from him. Don't worry; I know how to charm money out of old fools; I've done it so many times before. They're easy preys because they're lonely and kind and forgetful. You remember Old Sam who died last year? When I helped him to undress, I also cleaned up his billfold. By the time to pay me, he was so embarrassed to find his billfold empty that he promised to pay me double next time he sees me."

"You've told me this awful story a thousand times already," said Angie indifferently. "How could you be so freaking nasty to screw an old man like that?"

"Why not! He screwed me and I screwed him, that's fair." Linda's self-serving logical argument made Angie laugh.

"There is a big difference, you idiot," said Angie who wouldn't let Linda get away with what she considered a stupid argument. "He paid money to screw you, but you took his money to screw him. Can't you see?"

"Oh, don't be so finicky about such small things," Linda brushed off Angie's criticism casually. Not that Linda had forgotten the conversation she had with Randy; she liked his proposal very much. Not only would it give a new life for Angie but for her, too. But, having been growing up in two different screw-up families and had been a hooker for so long, she did not realize selling sex over the internet is also a dirty business, which is not that much different from her current profession. As to scam money out of Randy she saw nothing wrong with it as long as she had the intent to pay it back. Borrowing money isn't a crime, she thought.

After having seen the pitcher was empty, Angie took a big gulp of tequila right from the bottle, and then she asked apprehensively, "You mean we're going to scam Uncle Randy?"

"You got it right this time," answered Linda, feeling very proud.

"Oh, no," shouted Angie angrily, "you can't do this to him! Uncle Randy is a very nice man and I can't let you do this to him."

"We have no choice, Angie. After we've made the money, we'll pay him back with interest. You may say we just borrow money from him, all right?"

"No, it isn't all right, it's immoral! If you do, I'll tell Uncle Randy," said Angie, looking very serious and determined.

Linda, crestfallen, threw up her hands and said, "Well, I just want to help." Then, she walked out the apartment. But, minutes later, she came back and asked Angie if she wanted anything to eat.

"No, thank you. I'm not hungry," Angie said coldly.

But, as soon as the door was closed, she regretted the way she had treated Linda – too standoffish. For a moment she had an urge to open the door and call Linda to wait for her, but arrogance had forbidden her to do so. After all, Linda was the only intimate friend she had, and she should forgive Linda's manipulative behavior. She had a terrible childhood, abused and unloved, and she had been on her own roaming the streets since she was thirteen. In order to survive she had to do anything, moral or immoral, right or wrong, legal or illegal. She did not know the difference or simply did not care because nobody ever taught her anything. "One of these days, I'm going to give you little, unscrupulous, immoral scoundrel a good lesson on morality," Angie promised.

TWELVE

Fifteen minutes later Linda was back, carrying a plastic bag. She opened the refrigerator and poured herself a glass of milk. Then, she opened the bag and took out two foot-long turkey sandwiches from Galliano's Deli and started munching on one of them. Angie was watching silently, wondering how could a petite woman like Linda, who shopped regularly in the junior sections of department stores, consume two foot-long sandwiches. It is inconceivable, she thought, one of them ought to be for me. So she waited for the invitation, but it never came.

Without a word, Angie opened the refrigerator and poured herself a glass of milk, too, and sat down opposite to Linda, and then she reached for the other sandwich. But, before she could pick it up she was intercepted; Linda slapped her wrist and shouted, "Hey, that's my sandwich!"

"Can I have one? You can't eat all two!" begged Angie, childish smile on her face.

"You'd said you're not hungry. Six bucks if you want it."

When Linda opened her palm for the money, Angie smacked it with a loud "pop" and said angrily, "Here's six bucks for your lousy sandwich." With this childish act the ice between two good friends had melted away and they were talking again.

"I'm sorry, Linda," said Angie after having a big bite on the sandwich and washed it down with a gulp of milk. "I was a jerk, I shouldn't have got mad with you; you're my only friend. What can I do without you?"

"Me too, I'm sorry I'd made you mad. That's why I bought you a sandwich. I couldn't stand having you starving to dead because of me."

"You know, I've been thinking, if you're such a clever scammer, you shouldn't scam a nice old man like Uncle Randy, you should use your cleverness on a website designer. They're usually young and eager. If you can charm a fancy website out of them, that's all we need and we can start our own business right here right now. We don't have to live with two half-dead old men. You know what, if we move in with them it won't take long before we become two half-dead old women ourselves!"

"Hey, what do you mean "You, you, you"? You want me to do all the charming and you're just sitting here and sharing the profit?"

"That's not what I mean! But what can I do? I'm not a good charmer like you."

"Bullshit! If you're not a good charmer, how come that stingy Matt Dion gave you a mink coat, Roger Love gave you a diamond ring, and Johnny Dobb leaves you a hundred-dollar tips every time he comes?"

Suddenly, the two engaged in a fierce dirty-linen-washing war, throwing at each other tons of dirty linens. Not until they had run out of them and exhausted themselves in the fight and laughter, had they agreed to a ceasefire and a peace treaty – to charm a young website designer together.

"Shit! I've forgotten to let Uncle Randy know my decision," exclaimed Angie suddenly. "I'd promised him I'll get back to him in a few days. Now, Linda, what shall I tell him?"

"Just tell him our plan. If he has no objection, try to talk him into loaning us some money so that we don't have to charm the poor guy that hard. Besides, we need some money for Cowboy and for ourselves because we won't be able to work if we spend all our time on the damn charming."

"No! We can't tell him that," said Angie alarmingly. "He's an old-fashioned old man, I'm sure he won't approve."

"You dummy, you don't have to tell him what we're going to sell; just tell him we sell stuffs in the internet."

"What if he asks?" asked Angie doubtfully."

"Tell him that we'll sell anything that makes us money. Don't worry; old men don't know much about internet anyway. In case he find out later, it's no big deal; we're not selling our body as we're doing it now. It'll be a big improvement compared to what we're doing. He should be very happy for us."

It is true, Angie thought. It'll be a huge improvement. We don't have to stand at street corners to display ourselves like cheap dummies. We don't have to hustle and bargain with greasy jerks that pull up to us in their Goddamn cars and gawk at us as if they are buying a piece of meat. Best of all, we don't have to pay those bloodsucking pimps and abusive policemen protection money, and with the money saved I don't have to live in Daddy's house and to listen to his didactic speeches all the time. Yes, it will be hundreds and thousands times better than our current situation.

The more Angie dreamt about the possibilities of their future enterprise, the more excited she got. She wished they could start their new business this very minute. She was so excited that she called Uncle Randy right away.

"Uncle Randy, do you have time to meet me tonight, around ten? No, you can't, too late? Tomorrow afternoon?

Fine, the same place at three o'clock? Ok, I'll be there. Bye."

Angie was never anxious going to work; she procrastinated and was always late. Tonight was no exception. She'd have stayed home and not going to work had her fear of Cowboy was less than her aversion of her customers. Cowboy, the strong-armed manager of Angie and Linda's, wouldn't hesitate to suspense her supply of must-have dope or to kick her ass like footballs if she missed her weekly dues. She waited until Linda was gone before she reluctantly got herself ready for the night and went down to Three Corner. After two hours she was still standing on the sidewalk in front of the drugstore. Not because she was not desirable, no, she was still the most desirable hooker working in the area, but because she had intentionally jacked up her price so much that night that she'd priced herself out of competition. Angie was happy not to have any customer for the night though, because she didn't want any. The thought of being the owner of a successful enterprise had suddenly elevated her self-esteem; lowering herself to please unwanted customers had now become unacceptable. So, she went back to her apartment much earlier than usual.

When Linda came home three hours later (earlier than her normal), she was surprised to find Angie home. "Why are you home so early, no business?" she asked.

"I don't know why, but all of a sudden, I hate this shitty business so much. I hate the people here, I hate Three Corner, and I even hate my best customer and our apartment here. I really want to move the hell out of here."

"Strange, I got exactly the same feeling tonight! I never had this kind of feeling before; I was always happy to go down there to find an easy prey to screw him out of some dough. But not tonight, I found them disgusting, the whole Goddamn place is disgusting, and I know why."

"Why?" asked Angie, very anxious.

"Why," said Linda matter-of-factly, "we've been dreaming our new business the whole afternoon, which will be a hell of a lot better than the stinking one we're in now."

"I guess you're right."

"No guessing. I know I'm right. But, I don't know what we should do now. We don't like our jobs and we don't have the dough to start the new business. Even if we can charm a website out of a sucker engineer, it'll still take time to build up the business, and time is not on our side. One thing I do know, though, we can't sit here to starve. Besides, I won't be surprised that bastard Cowboy will come tomorrow to kick our asses. We'd better prepare to tell him we had food poisoning and diarrhea tonight."

"Shit, how could I forget that? He'd warned me many times: no money no Coke. What can I do without it?" Angie got up in frustration, flinging her hands like a spoiled child.

"I've told you to kick off that stuff, you just don't listen," said Linda, sounding like a big sister. "It's a very bad stuff; once you got hooked you're at the mercy of those son-of-a-bitch crocodiles. They'll eat you alive."

"Don't be a nag, please. Just tell me what to do."

"Let's move the hell out of here as soon as possible. I know Cowboy won't leave us alone. You know how vicious that fucking bastard is. Last time he'd almost broken your leg if I hadn't called the police."

"All right, all right, when I see Uncle Randy tomorrow, I'll ask if he will loan us some money."

"Also ask him if I can stay at his house for the next few days," said Linda, smiling slyly. She was very proud of herself that Angie had finally followed her lead. Her scare tactic did work this time.

THIRTEEN

Sitting side-by-side on a park bench with Uncle Randy, Angie dressed modestly this time compared to what she had worn to their last meeting when her provocative attire had embarrassed Uncle Randy. She could be very considerate sometimes if she wanted to, but most of the time, she wasn't concerned herself about other people's opinion of her.

"What's the matter with you, you look very tense?" asked Randy after he had been observing Angie suspiciously for a while. With his experience he knew she was up to something, otherwise she didn't need to have another meeting with him again. She could've just given him a straight answer over the phone.

"Nothing, really, we just have a little problem..." mumbled Angie inaudibly.

"Speak up. What kind of problem you girls have? Tell me, maybe I can help."

"Well—well, Linda and I had food poisoning—ate something bad, I guess, and we couldn't work for a few days, and our—our landlord comes to hassle us every day because we're behind our rent."

"I've told you to quit and move back home. We're sure we can find you something better to do."

"No need to, Uncle Randy. Linda said we can do business in the internet. Can make a lot of money and don't have to leave home."

"Really, what kind of business is that?" asked Randy skeptically. He had never heard of a business that you can make a lot of money without leaving home. True, he was old and not familiar with internet and did not even own a smart phone, but he had enough common sense and experience to tell a lie from a truth because he had been a businessman for more than forty years.

"Linda said we can sell things in the internet," said Angie enthusiastically. "All we need is a nice website."

"What sort of things will you gals sell?" Randy had already guessed what it was. What else can a hooker sells besides herself? That is all she knows and all she owns. But Randy was patient; he wanted to hear Angie telling him herself.

"Actually—actually we—we talk to our customers when they call, just talk to them that's all." Angie was stuttering and getting very fretful. She knew she must tell the truth if she wanted Uncle Randy's help, but, somehow, it was difficult to utter it out. Deep down in her heart she had a feeling that it was a devious business and Uncle Randy would definitely disapprove of it.

Noticing Angie's awkwardness, Randy was immensely amused. He was amazed that a twenty-two-year-old woman, who was a veteran in her profession, still could be this naïve and ignorant. Intending to embarrass her further, he asked, "Just talk? How can you make money by just talk?

"We'll charge their credit cards for the time we spend talking to them."

"I see, but why anyone wants to pay to talk to you, are you a lawyer, a marriage counselor, or a hospice comforter?"

"They're lonely, I guess. You know, there're a lot of lonely people in this world."

"I'm lonely too but I won't pay to talk to a gal on the phone. I can talk to as many people as I want to and it's free."

"Well, perhaps, they want to see our faces, too."

"What the hell they want to see your face for, they have hundreds and thousands of faces to see by just stepping out of their house or turning on the television set in their living room."

"Well—Linda said we can show them what they want to see," said Angie embarrassingly, her face started turning crimson.

"Now, I see, it's still the same kind of business," said Randy squarely.

"No, it isn't the same, Uncle Randy, it's on the phone and they can't do anything to us."

"Angie, Angie, it is the same kind of dirty business as you're in now, selling sex. I can understand Linda; she doesn't have a warm home and good parents to guide her. But you have a comfortable home and two nice parents, and you'd gone to school. How can you not see what you gals are doing and planning to do is wrong? Do you know you'd disappointed us, Angie?"

"Stop! Damn it, stop!" Angie shouted, so loud that people, who were watching their children play at the other end of the park, gazed in their direction. "I came today for help, not for your Goddamn lecture! What's wrong with our kind of business? Do we kill people? Do we cheat people? No! We're in service business. We provide services willingly and people pay for them willingly. What's wrong with that, eh?"

Either Randy could not answer or did not want to answer. He didn't say a word. He regretted he had touched Angie's hot-button, he should have known better that Angie was a very sensitive person and could hardly take criticism, even from her elders. The only sensible thing to do now was to let her blow the lid off of her boiling pot. But as he saw her pick up her purse and get ready to leave, he said softly, "Please sit down, Angie, let's talk a little more. Now, tell me how I can help."

"There's nothing more to talk about," said Angie defiantly and walked away, leaving Randy sitting on the park bench speechless, shaking his head in disbelief.

But Randy didn't leave the park; he sat there watching children play and he mumbled to himself: "Maybe she got a point. Yes, what's wrong with her profession? I don't see any difference between hers and other professions; they all provide services that people need and willing to pay for them. But, the service Angie provides is only her body while other professions provide a service of knowledge, of skill, of labor, and of time. Still, we have to use our body to acquire the knowledge, the skill, or to perform the labor...No, no, no, they are all the same, Angie is right. But, I know something is wrong. What...?" Sitting on the same park bench, Randy argued back and forth with himself for hours and still couldn't find a satisfactory answer for Angie's questions.

FOURTEEN

Linda knew what had happened at the meeting from the way Angie looked and acted – throwing her purse angrily onto the couch and kicking off her shoes with such a force that one of them hit the cupboard and shattered its glass door. She dared not say anything and she went back to polish her nails. Being a long-time friend and roommate of Angie's, she had found out the best way to make Angie talk was not to talk.

Distracting by the slamming of refrigerator door, crashing of dishes, and angry cussing, Linda looked up from time to time and saw Angie was still in bad mood, of which a big percentage was pretentious, intended to get Linda's attention.

Finally, running out of patience and failing to make Linda talk first, Angie suddenly asked, "Linda, how much dough do you have?"

"Not much, about sixty bucks. Why, you want some?" Linda said as casual and calm as she could.

"Shit! It's not enough to go down to TJ (Tijuana, Mexico). What shall we do now?"

"Why going down to TJ? Something's wrong?" Linda played dumb.

"We must get out of here before Goddamn Cowboy coming to kick our asses. Do you think you can borrow some dough from your friends or from some of your grandpa customers?"

"Angie, you're the only true friend I got, those phony bitches are only good for bullshitting; they won't give you a cent even if you beg. By the way, I thought we're going to move into Uncle Randy's place for a few days."

"Forget about that! It was a lousy idea anyway."

"Why, haven't you had a meeting with Uncle Randy? Have you asked him to let us—?"

Irritated, Angie cut in angrily and burst out like a broken fire hydrant, shooting up tons of dirty words and calling Randy from stupid old donkey to stubborn asshole. Linda went back to polish her nails, quietly waiting for the eruption to subside.

After banging the refrigerator door and throwing her purse a few more times, Angie came over standing before Linda and said angrily, "Aren't you interested in knowing what happened at the meeting?"

"Of course, I'm interested, but could I dare to ask you when you were in such a lousy mood?"

Angie went to fetch two cold beers from the refrigerator and handed one to Linda and that was her apology. Then, she told Linda what had happened.

"Why must you tell him what we're going to sell, you dumb idiot. Don't you know an old man like him won't support such an idea?"

"I don't think it's a bad idea, and that's what I told him, too," argued Angie.

"Well, you've blown it. Now, we'd better get ourselves busy figuring out how to deal with Cowboy, unless you want him to scratch hard on our backs." Cowboy's real name was Dennis Jaida but few people knew his real name; everybody called him Cowboy because he was big and tough and always wore cowboy boots, Wrangler pants and black leather jacket. He played football in high school and had dreamt of turning pro after graduation, but he turned pimping instead – after being booted out of police academy for bullying other cadets – because he was not good enough; he couldn't run or tackle, and he was good only at one thing – kicking footballs, which he found useful in his pimping business. To him, there was not much different between kicking footballs and kicking asses, they both gave him great satisfactions.

"We can claim we were sick, got food poisoning," Angie said dreamily. "Maybe he'll feel sorry for us and let us rest for a few days."

"The hell he will! You must have short memory! You don't remember how he'd beaten us up last time?"

"But, what other choice do we have? We have no dough going anywhere. Hey, are you sure you can't charm a few bucks out of those old fools of yours?"

"They aren't old fools, Angie, they're old foxes, and they can't be charmed as easily as those hungry young bucks."

"Can't you give it a try, please, we're freaking desperate now?"

"Do it in the middle of the day? No way! They won't take a drop until after work and they're sober and sneaky like a snake. Remember Old Bill? He was one of my regulars. He once tried to charm me into buying a fake diamond ring from him."

"Well, in that case, we better wear something thick and heavy and get ourselves ready to enjoy Cowboy's fucking boots."

"That's right," said Linda, depressed. "Now, we're at the mercy of Goddamn Cowboy." But she blamed Angie silently for walking away from Randy's help.

As expected, Cowboy pounded at their door that evening. Angie went quickly to the sofa and lay down with her face facing the back of the sofa, pretending sick. Linda, wrapped herself in a blanket, shuffled slowly to the door, pretending sick too.

"Where the hell you broads been?" hollered Cowboy the moment the door was opened. "Two nights in a row you didn't come down to work. You think you're on vacation or something!"

"We were sick, from food poisoning, those Goddamn greasy foods we ate at Olive Kitchen. The Goddamn diarrhea..." answered Linda, holding her belly and showing pain on her face. She was a damned good actress for a hooker and she'd tried very hard to be one, too. Unfortunately, to be an actress, even in adult movie business, one has to have a pretty face, a sexy figure, and a charming voice. And Linda had none of these; she was short and fat and had a face of over-ripe banana, full of freckles.

Cowboy pushed Linda aside and went straight to Angie and placed his cowboy boot on Angie's butt. He nudged her pugnaciously as he hollered at her, "You're sick too, uh?"

"Ouch! Stop it!" Angie yelled back without turning.

"Please don't, Cowboy, Angie's really in a bad fix," pleaded Linda when she saw him going to nudge Angie again.

"Sick? My foot! She needs Coke and a good spanking," shouted Cowboy. Then, he grabbed a ruler from a nearby table and started hitting Angie left and right, so savagely that Angie rolled off the sofa and screamed for help. When Linda jumped in to pull Cowboy away from Angie, she was shoveled aside and she lost her balance and fell on a coffee table that bruised her left eye. Not until the landlord came to interfere and threatened to call the police that Cowboy ceased the brutal beating. But, before he left he issued a stern warning to the two girls: "If I don't see you broads come down to work tomorrow night, I'll come back here to beat the shit out of you both."

After Cowboy had left, Linda went into the bathroom and cried out seconds later: "Shit, look at me! How can I go to see Randy like this?"

Angie came quickly and saw Linda's left eye blackened and swollen like a ripe plum. "Does it hurt?" Angie asked and touched it with the tip of her finger.

"Ouch! Don't do that!" Linda screamed, pushing Angie's hand away.

"I think you'd better go see a doctor."

"No! I want to see Randy!" said Linda angrily. "But, how can I see him now with my eye looks like this!"

"Who's Randy? Do I know him?"

"It's your Goddamn Uncle Randy! I want to ask him if he will let me move in with him for a while."

"You crazy fool, you must be dreaming! You're a hooker, don't forget, Linda, and you expect him to take you in? What would his neighbors and friends think of him, huh?"

"I got no choice. I've got to try unless we want that son-of-a-bitch beat up us again."

"Do as you like but I tell you, Uncle Randy is an old-timer; he won't accept hookers."

"After I move in with him, I won't be a hooker anymore. I'll get a regular job and become a nice girl again."

"Good luck with your dream!" said Angie. After that she said no more.

At that time, they heard the pounding on the door again, which made them jump on their feet with terror, thinking it was Cowboy again, coming back for more. Then, they heard the landlord's voice: "Are you girls okay?" He came to claim his reward – that was what he expected – for saving the girls from the hands of a tyrant. He was a wicked, filthy old scum and forever single, for he was unwilling to share what he owned but loved to share what other people owned. He had been working at a local bar as a bartender for most of his adult years and saved enough money to buy this six-unit apartment half a block from Three Corner. He bought it not entirely with his own savings though, but with the generous profit sharing that he offered himself arbitrarily, without guilty conscience and without the consent or knowledge of the owner. He helped himself every shift a percentage of the gross proceeds from the mute cash register. He had having an eye on Angie and Linda for a long time, hoping the proximity to them as their landlord would have certain advantage. When he saw them his greedy eyes went over their whole bodies, showing his true nature. In their presence he was superficially respectful and courteous, but in their backs he spat out scornful remarks. He regularly did them favors by letting them stall on their rents or by coming over to fix a leaky faucet or something, expecting like an servile dog that the girls would show their appreciations by offering him a piece of meat, but always he got nothing more than a disappointingly cool 'thank you'.

"Hi, girls, are you okay now? I'm glad I was home to kick him out of here, otherwise, you girls would've been in a deep shit."

"Sure would, Mr. Underwood. Thank you very much for your help," said Linda as she opened the door for him with a charming smile.

"You're very welcome. Is there anything else I can do for you girls?"

"No, thank you," Linda said as she started walking the landlord to the door.

"Oh, yes, can you lend us some money, just for a week and we'll pay you back with interest." Angie had been silently watching them playing the polite game and it amused her greatly. She never liked the landlord much and was always cool to him, but this time, out of desperation, she was forced to lower herself and be humble.

Their landlord was arrested at the door; he turned to look at Angie, surprised, and said, "I don't want interest."

"Then, what do you want?" asked Angie, equally surprised. She was wondering: a greedy old cheapskate doesn't want any interest? Strange!

"I want you for one night," said the landlord boldly and unashamedly, which astounded both girls. Angie's face changed color instantly and was about to trade insults with him.

"We'll think about it and let you know later," said Linda quickly as she gently pushed the landlord out with plenty of thanks and half-hearted promises.

"Why are you so nice to that dirty old skunk?" asked Angie angrily. "You should've thrown him out!"

"Angie, you still have a lot to learn. To handle a mean snake like him you have to be very careful; he can bite you and make your life miserable if he doesn't like you. Besides, we're behind on his rent already. He can evict us if he wants to."

Angie had to admit that this time Linda was right, she was always right in a situation like this; she got a cool head which was necessary to survive in the mean streets of Lake Eleazy.

"I'm going out, I'll be back before dinner," said Linda before she left the apartment.

"Where are you going? Can't you try borrowing some money from some of your regulars? Please!"

Linda stopped at the door for a moment, and then she turned back and said, "I'll try but will you spend a night with that old skunk if I fail?"

"No! Not for a million bucks!" exclaimed Angie.

"If you're not willing, how about moving in with Uncle Randy?" Cunning Linda tried to trap Angie into an agreement; she knew Angie wouldn't touch the old skunk with a ten-foot pole.

"Ok, fine," said Angie, rather reluctantly.

"Promise?"

"I promise."

FIFTEEN

The first person Linda approached was Hot Pepper because she knew him well; she was one of the dealers for his miracle supplement, HPSE. Hot Pepper was a gregarious big man with a hot temper to match the product he was selling. When he saw Linda coming, he opened his arms and lifted the petite woman in the air, showing the happiness of a father playing with his child. But, when she asked him for a loan, his facial expression changed instantly, from joyous to harsh, and he refused her, saying: if you need money, sell more HPSE. Linda knew better not to say anything but left quietly.

Sean Otis, a regular client of Linda and the owner of a grocery store, was next. He, too, hurried to greet Linda when he saw her coming and asked quite loudly, "How can I help you, Miss?" Linda was amazed, wondering what's wrong with Sean, greeting her like a stranger. She was going to protest when she saw him wink at her and followed by a barely audible whisper: "My wife is here, go, I'll call you later."

Now, Linda understood, so she whispered back, "Can you lend me two hundred bucks?"

"Please go!" Sean whispered again before he turned to help another customer.

Only after Linda and the other customer were gone that Sean's wife asked, "What's that girl wanted, you two were whispering?"

"Oh, that crazy girl, she asked if we can sell her a bag of rice on credit, said her husband had gambled all their money away."

"Why didn't you give her some? Poor thing, her family will have nothing to eat."

"Don't feel sorry for her kind. Can't you tell she's a bad girl?"

"She looks fine to me except her clothes a little…you know what I mean."

By eight o'clock Linda had visited four more regular clients and still couldn't borrow a cent from them. They all had convenient excuses for not lending her money. Except one, who took out a few dollars and some loose changes and said, "This is all I have, you take it." Linda didn't take it. She felt insulted.

Dejected and hungry, she went in a burger joint to have a cheeseburger and a large Coke, trying to figure out what to do next. She and Angie needed money for sure and needed it fast, and there was no hope of getting it. While she was pondering whether she should go back to work or should try a few more former customers, she suddenly thought of Uncle Randy and she decided to pay him a visit.

Linda parked her car at the curb in front of Randy's house. It was only nine-thirty in the evening but the street was ghostly empty. By the brightness in the living room, she knew Randy was still up. But she was hesitating, debating whether she should step out of the car or go home. Angie's remark was still clearly ringing in her ears, and she did not want to create any trouble for Randy because of her shameful occupation. Even though she dressed inconspicuously, the street was dimly lit, and Randy's front yard was barely illuminated by a tiny light above the front door, Linda still worried about being seen. After sitting in the car for a few more minutes to make sure there was no one in the street, she got out and walked stealthily and nimbly like a mouse to Randy's house.

"Who's this?" asked Randy when he heard someone knocking at the door.

"Mr. Gibbs, it's me, Linda."

"Who?"

"Linda, Angie's friend."

Recalling Linda was the girl Angie had sent to see him last week he hurried to open the door. "Why come so late, Angie sent you again? Oh, my God, What happened to your eye?" exclaimed Randy when he saw Linda's blackened eye.

"I'm terribly sorry to trouble you this late, Mr. Gibbs. May I come in to talk to you for a minute?" said Linda forthrightly.

"It's quite all right. Come on in," said Randy. But when he saw Linda looking at him with a strange expression, he suddenly realized he was in his pajama. "Please have a seat; I'll be right back," he said and left the living room awkwardly. When Randy came back, he had changed into a long-sleeved dress shirt and a pair of perfectly-ironed khakis, and black socks, too. He could never receive visitors but Rob bare-footed. "Not respectful for my guest," he always explained. "Now, tell me how you got your eye messed up like this," he demanded as if Linda were his child, extremely concerned.

"Oh, it's an accident; I bumped onto a door."

"Wait a minute; I think I've something that will help heal the wound."

"Please don't bother, Mr. Gibbs," Linda said quickly. "It'll heal itself at no time. I came tonight to ask you a question."

"Yes, I just want to ask you why you came to me this late. Something urgent or is it about Angie?" Randy smelt something fishy but he couldn't pinpoint what it was. A prostitute with whom he had met only once came to ask a question at bed-time hour, how could he not get nervous?

"Not really, I want—want to know what you'd told me last week still counts?"

"What exactly I'd told you? I've forgot." Randy started feeling uneasy, wondering what he'd promised Linda.

"You said: if I help you save Angie, you'll try to save me too. Do you still mean it?"

"Oh, yes, I remember I did say that. Of course, my word is still good."

"Even Angie doesn't want to be helped?"

"Yes, even that," Randy said unwaveringly. "Now, tell me what makes you think Angie doesn't want our help."

"You see, Angie must have money to support her bad habits."

"What bad habits she has?"

"You don't know? She's hooked on heroine."

"I suspect she is but I'm not sure."

"Yes, sir, she is, for a long time now. I've asked her many times to quit that awful stuff but she just won't listen. Angie is a very stubborn girl, you know. I doubt she'll quit her job; she's still young and making good money. That's the reason why I came tonight to ask you this question: do you still want to save me if I can't help you save Angie?"

"Absolutely! I always keep my words."

"What do you want from me in return, Mr. Gibbs? I mean for your help." asked Linda bluntly and her suspicion reflected in her tone. She assumed Randy's generous help came with a hefty price, for she had yet met a person who would do her a favor without wanting something in return.

Stunned by this kind of ungrateful and disrespectful question, Randy felt insulted and his face was instantly inflamed. He would have hollered and ordered Linda to get out had he not suddenly remembered she was a runaway, unwanted and unloved by her family, and had been practically growing up in the sinful streets of Lake Eleazy. Poor gal, how could she know better? Nobody ever gave her anything for free, he thought. And with this thought Randy's heart turned soft and his voice tender. He said, lowering his voice as low as he could manage, "My dear Linda, do you think I'm one of your customers, always wants something from you? You don't believe I'll help you for free, do you? Let me tell you now, my dear, I don't want anything from you, zero, nothing! You got it? I want to help you because I feel sorry for you to have such lousy parents, and you've demonstrated to me that you're a good girl. But, I don't blame you; you've been around bad people for too long that you think all people are bad like them. Let me tell you, there are more good people in this world than bad people. You'll see if you give yourself a chance to know them."

Linda was listening attentively and tears started running down her cheeks. She was moved not only by Randy's kind words and genuine concerns, but also by his mentioning of her wretched family background, which had reopened the old wounds that had hurt her so much. Every one of Randy's words seemed as if they were new vocabularies, of which she had never heard before. But they were comforting words, encouraging words, so encouraging that her tears was now pouring like rain and she felt ashamed that she had offended the person who seemed to be really cared about her. Only after she had stopped sobbing and dried her eyes with the tissues given to her, she said haltingly, "I'm terribly sorry, Mr. Gibbs, I was a fool, I was wrong; I thought you're one of those phony kind-faced bastards."

"What kind-faced bastards?"

"Bad people who..." Linda started sobbing again.

"What bad people?"

"Those who prey on us naïve runaway children, they put on a kind face and pretend they are from charity organizations, out there to help us, to save us from bad creditors. But they are the bad creditors; they'd bring us back to their apartments, give us food and ask us a lot of questions about our backgrounds. When they find out we are deserted children and nobody give a damn about us, then, they'd show their real faces; they'd get us drunk or stoned and rape us and make us hookers..."

Randy listened quietly but his face had been changing color fast, from healthy tan to angry purple. "You f— son-of-a-bitch," he burst out suddenly, which startled Linda to hear such angry words from the mouth of an old gentleman like Randy. She thought only illiterate people would speak like that. But she didn't know her story had infuriated Randy, not at her but at those low-down kind-faced bastards. Randy had never ever been this angry before, so angry that he could have killed them.

"Sorry for scaring you, Linda; I shouldn't have got so angry like this. But, how about Angie, did she get hurt, too?

"No, because she had me to protect her and she stayed with me. Most girls aren't that lucky though, bad people get them hooked on drugs so that they have complete control of them. Angie is pretty much in the same situation."

"I see, so Angie is under their control because she needs their drugs. Is that right?"

"You may say that."

"Have you told Angie the truth about her father?"

"No, I haven't. You told me not to, remember?"

"Good, now let me tell you what to do when you get back there. I'm pretty sure she can be saved," said Randy. Then, they spent the next half an hour going over their strategies.

It was almost midnight when Linda came home, but Angie was still up and still in bad mood. She was mumbling and cussing so loud that Linda could hear her even before she opened the door.

"How much dough you got from them?" Angie asked the moment Linda walked in the apartment.

"Forget about them! I couldn't squeeze a dime out of those cold-hearted cheapskates."

"Now, what shall we do? We can't go down to TJ and no place to hide?"

"Move back home, Angie, we got no other choice."

"I won't!"

"You'd promised me you would if I couldn't borrow the money."

"I change my mind."

"So, you aren't going to honor your fucking promise, is that right? All right, fine, I move out by myself then." Linda was really mad and she flung herself on the sofa, puffing. You could see smoke coming out her nostrils.

After that they ignored each other's presence as if they were alone. Linda went to bed happily, humming her favorite tunes; and Angie went to bed touchily, making a lot of annoying noises.

Next morning, Linda woke up first and started humming softly again while she was preparing breakfast. Angie, annoyed, pulled the blanket over her head, exercising her silent protest. But she could not keep silent any longer when she heard first and then saw later Linda open drawers and suitcases and begin packing. "Where are you going?" she asked.

"Move to Uncle Randy's house," answered Linda, happiness in her voice.

"No kidding, he must be getting senile, got conned so easily." Angie was jealous; her remark was full of mockery.

"I have no need to con him. He's a very kind man and I respect him a lot," retorted Linda, mocking back.

Angie said no more, just watching Linda packing. At first, she thought Linda's packing was a sham, trying to tease her, but by the time Linda walked out of the door with two full suitcases, she knew it was not a joke. She jumped out of bed, ran after Linda and grasped her hand and asked loudly, loud enough to wake up their neighbors, "Linda, you're really leaving, leaving me alone here?"

Linda dropped her two suitcases and said resolutely, "I've told you I'll move out, haven't I? If you want another spanking, go ahead; it's you choice but not mine! I don't want another one like this." As she said she pointed to her swollen eye and bent down to lift her suitcases.

Angie stopped her, holding tight to her arm, and pleaded pitifully, "You can't leave me to face Cowboy by myself, Linda. We've been together for a long time, please help me! Don't be mean."

"Then, pack up and go with me!"

"I can't!"

"You can't or you don't want to?"

"I just can't!" cried Angie.

"Why, you got to tell me if you want my help," said Linda in a voice almost like commanding.

"I got to have money."

"For what, buying dopes?

"Yes!" said Angie crossly. "Even if I don't need money to buy dope, I still need it to eat!"

"Your father can support you for a while."

"Are you kidding me? No way will he support a junkie daughter!"

"He will. Uncle Randy told me."

"I see! You went to see Uncle Randy. Why you lied to me, said you were going to borrow money from friends." Angie was furious.

"I didn't lie. I did go out borrowing money, but when I couldn't borrow any from those cheapskates, I went to see Uncle Randy, hoping he would lend us some."

"Are you sure, Uncle Randy told you that?"

"I don't see any reason why Uncle Randy wants to lie to me. He asked me to tell you that your father wants you home."

"No way! I'd rather be a whore for the rest of my life than going home. You have no idea how difficult he is to live with. You're expected to do everything according to his rules, and he got so many Goddamn rules!"

"Angie, you don't know how lucky you are to have parents who really care about you. I envy you because nobody ever gave a damn about me. I considered it very fortunate if my parents didn't beat the shit out of me. You have no idea how my life was like before I ran away from home. Let me tell you, it was ten times worse than being homeless. You know how horrible it was for a runaway girl like you and me – no money, no friends and no place to sleep, and we were constantly frightened because there were so many dangerous people out there trying to take advantage of us. You were luckier because when you ran away you had me to take care of you."

What Linda said had helped Angie remember all the pleasant memories of being raised like a princess by her devoted parents. She remembered all the Barbie dolls and the beautiful dresses and shoes her parents lavished on her on special occasions and on not-so-special occasions. She remembered they always let her order whatever she wanted while most parents restricted their kids' choice to kid's menu. Yes, she also remembered how Linda cared for and protected her like a big sister all these years when she was the most vulnerable, and without Linda she couldn't have possibly survived in the mean streets of Lake Eleazy. Indeed, she was deeply indebted to her.

"Are you sure my father wants me back?" she asked Linda again.

"Sure! Would I lie to you? Hurry up, pack your stuffs and let's get the hell out of this shitty place."

Angie did not move; she stood there, as still as Linda's two suitcases; she was hesitating as if she was making a choice between live or die. Finally, she asked timorously, "Does my Daddy know that I'm a junkie?"

"That I don't know," said Linda, "but does it matter?"

"Sure, it does! He may not want me back if he knows."

"Let me ask Uncle Randy, he may know."

SIXTEEN

At Randy home Linda related Angie's concern to Randy who was not sure himself, so he called Rob Taylor over to his house.

"Do you know Angie is a drug addict?" asked Randy.

"I suspect she is. Who would want to be a hooker if she isn't hooked?"

"I'm not," protested Linda who was hurt by Rob's remark which implied all hookers are drug addicts.

"You are not?" asked Rob incredulously, part surprised and part embarrassed.

"No, Linda is not. She never has been," said Randy. "Linda was a very smart girl. She just had a bad break, that's all." Then, Randy told Rob what Linda had told him. How she had a dysfunctional family with an uncaring mother and an alcoholic stepfather who had sexually abused her when she was only a child. How she had run away from home because of that and how she had survived as a homeless child in the dangerous streets of Lake Eleazy, where pimps and drug pushers ruled the streets and where the porno industry made it the adult movie capital of the world. He also told Rob how street smart Linda was, who had avoided getting hooked by performing a clever act to deceive her manager – feigning an allergic reaction to the drug: hallucinating and acting crazy, which rendered her unproductive as a money tree.

Randy's account of her made Linda fill with pride and self-pity, a mixed emotion that she tried very hard to contain. But Rob couldn't contain his; he had to use a handkerchief to dry his eyes periodically. He felt sorry for Linda but sorrier for his daughter. Linda's story enabled him, for the first time, to realize the miserable life of a runaway. The mere thought that his daughter must have been going through the same horrendous hell and still in it rendered him speechless. He hung his head and busily wiping his eyeglasses with a handkerchief. How could I be so cruel to kick her out of our house? She didn't run away, I forced her to…Rob scolded himself silently, remorse, guilt and sadness could be read upon his face.

Having witnessed an old man display emotion like this, Linda felt uncomfortable and she said, trying to easy Rob's pain, "I've try to get Angie to quit that awful stuff but she has a hard time doing it. She has been doing drug for a long time and she told me Johnny Stewart had introduced her to it…"

"That son-of-a-bitch, he'd really fucked her up!" barked Rob. But right away he apologized, "Execute me, please forgive my language."

Linda did not mind. She did not think it was a big deal because she had heard much worse than that all the time and even she, herself, talked like that very often. But Randy was the one who was shocked. For more than thirty years as Rob's neighbor and good friend, he'd never seen him getting mad, much less using foul language, especially before a female. In order to avoid further embarrassment, he veered from the subject by saying: "We can help her to quit but we have to get her home first. Linda, do you think you can talk her into it?"

"I don't know. Angie still worries Mr. Taylor may throw her out again."

"Tell her don't worry; I guarantee everything will be all right," said Randy. Then, he turned and asked Rob, "Can you control your temper a bit and give her time to change? This is our last chance to save her."

"I'll try, provided that she won't take drugs and use foul language anymore. You know, I hate people use profanity."

"I know. I've never heard you cussing, have you, Linda?" asked Randy as he winked at her.

"Never!" answered Linda positively, but a sly smile on her face belied her sincerity.

After Rob had finally realized what they were laughing at, he joined them at once to cover up his embarrassment.

After Linda left, the two old friends had a long conversation about the two girl's situation. Randy was very happy that Linda had come and was willing to help, and with her help he was pretty sure things would work out the way he had planned. But Rob had a mixed emotion; on one hand he was excited about the likelihood of his daughter's coming home and having a second chance of starting all over again, but on the other hand, he worried they might not be able to live together in harmony. She just had too many bad habits and problems of which he doubted could change overnight. So, he asked, "Do you think this is a good idea?

"What idea?"

"The idea of getting Angie home, we may not be able to reform her; she got so many problems, the drugs, the alcohol, her friends, lifestyle..."

"Isn't that the reason we have to save her? Let's not worry about her problems yet. Right now, let us get her home first, one thing at a time."

"But...I just worry we can't get along. You know my temper, I may not be able to tolerate her and she may run away again. I can't let her do it to me all over again, you understand?"

"Believe me, she won't. Between Linda and me, I think we can straighten her out. Linda is a good girl, pretty smart and she loves Angie and she is Angie's only true friend out there, and Angie will listen to her."

"But that Linda is a wild card herself, a bad influence, and I think Angie's runaway has a lot to do with her."

"Perhaps she was but no more, she's my little good girl now and she'll listen to me."

"Really?" said Rob in disbelief.

"No really, you'll see." Randy said with an assertive smile.

SEVENTEEN

It was late afternoon when Linda came back and she saw Angie was napping on the couch. No packing was evidenced; obviously she had no intention to leave.

"Wake up, Angie. We better hurry, Cowboy may come soon."

Angie turned around and stretched her arms lazily and asked, "What time is it?"

"Almost five, you haven't packed yet?"

"Why pack?"

"You're going home! Hurry up, will you?"

"I've told you, I'm not moving."

"Angie, get up!" Linda bent down, trying to pull Angie up. "I've a long talk with Randy and your father. They said they will help you kick off the stuff and your father had promised Randy not to get mad with you."

Pushing on the couch with one hand and letting Linda pull her up with the other, Angie looked at Linda with two half-closed eyes and said, "Look at me, Linda, I'm sick without the stuff. How can I face them in this condition, huh? You go. I'm staying here. Maybe Cowboy will give me some if I promise him going to work tonight."

"Angie, please listen to me," Linda begged, holding Angie's hand, "don't worry how you look. They understand and they'll help you overcome this. You'll die if you don't quit that stuff. You must let us help you, Angie, please!"

"You go, Linda, don't worry about me; I'm dead long time ago."

"I won't go if you don't!" Linda said resolutely.

"Why, Uncle Randy is a nice man and he'll provide you with a nice warm home. Isn't it what you always want?"

"Yes, that's what I dream for all my life and Uncle Randy is the kind of father I always want to have. But, Angie, you're my only friend and I consider you my sister, the only family I have, and I can't leave you here to suffer, to die alone. If to die is what you want, let's die together, right here, right now."

Angie did not want to die, only the severe sufferings caused by the side effects of withdrawal that had depressed her, making her to give up on herself. But letting Linda give up her future because of her she could not do. That would be too selfish and she was not a selfish person. Now, after hearing Linda's passionate pleading and her willingness to sacrifice herself for her, Angie, like having a hormone shot in her arm, was energized.

"Okay, Big Sister, would you help me pack?" asked Angie after she let Linda pulling her up.

"Of course, Little Sister, let's get going."

The two, working together, busily but happily packed for an hour. After they had put the last baggage in the trunk of Angie's car, they planned to go up the apartment to leave the keys and a note for the landlord, and to finish the bottle of wine in the refrigerator. But, when they were crossing the street, they saw Cowboy's car coming; they could recognize it from far away because it had a pair of buffalo horns mounted on its hood. They darted back and got in the car, sitting low. After they saw him going into the apartment building, Linda quickly went back to her car and took off, followed by Angie.

They did not go straight to Randy's house; they stopped at a restaurant in Marietta instead. They needed to talk over a few things first. When they got out of their cars and were still in the parking lot, they could not help but laughed.

"Can you imagine what Cowboy will do when he finds us gone with the wind?"

"He'll kick the door down for sure," said Angie, still laughing.

"I bet he is now enjoying himself," lamented Linda. "Kicking off his Goddamn cowboy boots and putting his lousy feet on the coffee table, drinking our wine and munching on our cold pizza, and watching his favorite Goddamn cowboy movies. Oh, Angie, do you still have the keys to the apartment? We have to write a note and mail the keys back to the landlord."

"I have them here," said Angie, pulling out a chain of keys from her purse. "How about Cowboy, he won't give up that easy. He'll hunt us down for sure."

"We'll be all right if we stay home for a while and don't go to Lake Eleazy."

"For how long we have to hide?" asked Angie grumpily. The idea of not be able to go out displeased her.

"A few weeks, I hope, but we can't go back to Lake Eleazy for a long time unless we want to have our asses kicked again."

Angie had no more to say and her mood was clearly unhappy, and added to her unhappiness, Linda cautioned her during dinner that she should be careful with her language and temper. "Old people don't like cussing and quick temper. You should dress modestly, for provocative clothes invites contempt and makes making friends difficult. You should obey them, at least give them a chance to prove that they were right." All these teachings were not Linda's own creation, of course, they were Randy's. She just repeated what Randy had told her to tell Angie. By now, Linda had full confidence in Randy; his strategy and the words that he taught Linda to persuade Angie worked effectively. Angie did agree to return home.

Angie was at a lost by Linda's second-handed teaching; she wondered from where Linda learned how to speak like that, all of a sudden talking decency, etiquette, manner, and personal appearance. "Okay! You sound like my father," said Angie.

"I just want to help you get used to it before you move back home. I know the two old guys don't like a lot of things about young people, especially us. We must try to please them if we want to get hold some of their money."

"You Goddamn phony, always think about money. I must warn you: don't try to scam them, I won't allow."

Before they left the restaurant and drove to Randy's house, Linda reminded Angie again: "We're lucky to have someone truly loves us. This is our only chance, Angie, please don't blow it, you hear?"

"Yes sir. Big Sister."

EIGHTEEN

Randy and Rob were in Randy's living room watching TV. They had been waiting anxiously ever since Linda called to tell them Angie had agreed to come home. They had a long conversation about what to do with the two girls. They planned to enroll Angie into a rehabilitation center and find Linda a waitress job at Stagecoach Inn. Most important of all, they agreed to work together and be very patient with them. They both knew that to transform two hookers who had been in association with so many lowest of the lows of society into two decent ordinary girls would not be easy.

When the two girls arrived, they came out to help them with their luggage, Randy carried Linda's into his house and Rob carried Angie's into his. They had prearranged this so that Rob and his daughter could have the opportunity to reconcile in privacy, without the awkwardness of doing it in the presence of other people. However, being separated for so long and in hostile relationship, a sudden reunion was everything but comfortable.

They stood silently facing each other and both found no word to break the ice. No hugs and no kisses and not even say "Hi" to each other. But, all of a sudden, as if Angie had been kicked behind both knees, she dropped down on her knees before her father, begging for forgiveness. Rob Taylor did not expect his daughter, who was as stubborn as a mule and had never apologized for her wrongs, would do this. He was caught by surprise and did not know what to do, but after a moment of hesitation, he bent down to pull her up. Spontaneously, Angie threw both arms around her father neck and burying her face in his chest, crying shamelessly, "Oh, Daddy, I missed you! I missed home!" The impending emotion of seven long years of hate and remorse was just too powerful a force for a broken girl to withstand.

"I know. It's all right now." Rob said as he patted gently on his daughter's back. Silently they hugged for a long time, enjoying the warmth and sweetness only kinship could have provided.

At Randy's house next door, things unfolded differently but not less dramatically and lovingly. After Randy showed Linda her room and the rest of the house, he said to her: "Linda, this is your home now, feel free and make yourself comfortable. You hear?"

"Thank you, Uncle Randy. Oh, can I call you just Uncle?"

"Sure, you may call me Daddy if you like. We have no children; I'll treat you like one if you want me to."

"I'd like it very much, Daddy. Thank you for giving me a lovely home. I've never felt I had a home before. I never knew what love feels like until now. Thank you, thank you very much, Daddy." Linda gave Randy a big hug and a kiss on his cheek.

"On a second thought, Linda, call me Uncle is better. It will be very strange for me to have a daughter all of a sudden. You know how people think."

"Ok, Uncle."

"Come, how about have a drink to celebrate?"

"I wonder how Angie and her father are…"

"Don't worry, they'll be fine. Oh, let me call them over to join us. We can celebrate together."

No other people in the world were happier than these four. Randy opened a bottle of wine and brought out a platter of assorted cheese and nuts. They talked only about the future, about a plan to take a long vacation together as a family and other cheerful things. When Linda and Angie brought up the problems they were facing, Randy would brush them aside by saying, "Those problems can wait. Let's take a vacation and enjoy ourselves for a while first, to catch up all those lost time. You know what, by the time we come back, those problems might not be there anymore."

NINETEEN

To Angie, living with her father was difficult even though they both tried their best to accommodate each other. There were just too many differences between daughter and father; among them was the generation gap – the new culture against the old. Angie liked to dress fashionably in sexy outfits and used foul language, of which her father found it difficult to approve. But this was minor and something could be tolerated in comparison to the differences in opinion about prostitution and pornography.

Their differences had been exacerbated proportionally by the length of their separation, which made friendly conversation and harmonious living impossible. Her father got up and retired to bed early, and conducted his daily activities almost exactly the same way, day in and day out. Angie, on the contrary, had no daily routines; her schedules were as flexible as her mind was inflexible. She might go to bed at four o'clock in the morning and got up at two in the afternoon, she might go out for a whole day or stayed in bed twenty-four hours, and she might eat breakfast in the evening and dinner in the morning. As a result, they seldom saw and much less talked to each other even though they lived under the same roof.

But all these differences were minor problems compared to her drug addiction. During her two month's stay at the rehab center, Angie was doing unexpectedly well. With the encouragement from Linda and the understanding from Uncle Randy and her father, she had little trouble quitting the stuff and she was quite happy in general. It was after her discharge from the center and a visit to a friend in Lake Eleazy that her old problems returned. She started going out more often and increasingly she came home rather late, and sometimes not at all. When her father questioned her, she would simply reply in the same defiant way as before: "It's none of your business."

Rob was very disappointed and his frustrations intensified as time passed. So many times he had nearly lost his temper and would have kicked her out again if he had not remembered his promise to Randy.

Randy and Linda had no knowledge about this; Randy thought everything went well next door and Linda was too busy with her new job that she scarcely found the time to see Angie. She was very happy at work and at home. She and Randy got along beautifully. The only regret they both had was that they met a bit too late. Only if they had met when Linda first ran away from home, Linda would have saved herself from the misery of living in the streets among treacherous people, would have got a degree and thus a much higher paying job, and Randy and his wife would have adopted her and have someone call them Daddy and Mommy.

For some reason Rob hadn't told Randy and Linda the problems he had had with his daughter until the night when she came home with a black eye and a split lip. He asked but got no answer; she rushed into her room and shut the door. Panicked, Rob went and banged on Randy's door urgently. "What should I do now with my Angie, she acts up again just like before?" he asked fretfully.

"What's the matter?" Randy and Linda asked concurrently. They were having an after dinner drink and watching a soap opera together at the time.

"Angie was hurt, somebody had beaten her up," said Rob. "Linda, please go find out what had happened, quick!"

"I bet it is Cowboy again," said Linda before she left.

After Linda left, Rob told Randy the whole story and when he finished he asked again, "What should we do now?"

"We should go talk to the rehab people tomorrow. They may be able to help."

Half an hour later, Linda came back and conformed that it was indeed Cowboy who had beaten up Angie. What happened was, when Angie went to a friend's birthday party in Lake Eleazy, Cowboy was there, too. When he saw Angie come in, he grabbed her by the wrist and dragged her back out to the front yard and asked punitively, "Where the hell have you been, I've been looking all over for you two fucking boards?"

"Linda and I went down to Mexico and got stuck there for a while." Angie lied poorly; even a child could tell she wasn't telling the truth.

"You lousy liar, you think you can get away not working and not paying me?" Whack! Whack! Cowboy started slapping her left and right with his giant palm, and Angie was screaming at the top of her lungs for help. She would have been beaten to death had the other partygoers not heard her scream and come out to restraint the furious Cowboy. Naturally, nobody called the police, for it made no difference one way or the other; Cowboy was an ex-cop and he still had a lot of clout in this sin city.

Randy and Rob went to the rehab center early the next day and they were directed to see the director of the center. After they had told him about Angie's case, the director said, "Oh, don't worry. She's a smart gal; she'll overcome this. It's quite normal for addicts to have relapses. The misery of quitting is dreadful, which tends to depress them and weaken their minds. It takes courage and determination to face it and it takes time for them to cut off their old ties. What we should do now is to keep her busy and keep her away from her old environment."

"We tried to get her a waitress job but she said the pay is too low and she doesn't like serving people," said Randy helplessly and Rob nodded in agreement.

"Try to find her something she likes to do, then."
"We had but, you see, she has no degree and no other experiences except—." Randy stopped short. He couldn't tell the director that Angie was a hooker in front of her father.

The director understood, so he simply said, "I may have a job for her. It doesn't pay a lot but it's a very challenging one. I think Angie may like it."

"What kind of job?" Randy and Rob asked simultaneously, very excited.

"Working here at the center as an assistant motivator, she can help us to convince other addicts to quit. Most of our motivators were former addicts. No better person than an ex-addict for that kind of job because they have been experiencing the same problems and they understand each other. Also, to motivate others is a very effective process of self-motivation. Tell her to call me if she's interested."

"We thank you very much. Thank you." They both said and left, very excited and grateful.

But their excitement had diminished considerably when they were half way home. "I have been thinking, Rob, we better let Linda do the persuasion. You know, Angie is very proud and very stubborn, I don't think she'll take the job if she knows we got it for her. We'll discuss this tonight with Linda, perhaps she has a better idea. For the meantime don't say anything to Angie."

Rob nodded, dejected like a punctured balloon.

TWENTY

Well prepared after having a fairly long discussion with Randy and Rob, Linda knocked on Angie's bedroom door and called out, "Angie, open the door. It's me, Linda."

When there was no answer, Linda twisted open the door and went in. Angie was lying in bed with her face facing the wall. When Linda tried to pull her up, she resisted and started sobbing.

"What's the matter, Angie?"

"What's the matter? Can't you see?" Angie suddenly turned around to face Linda.

"I can see all right," said Linda somberly. What she saw in front of her – a deplorable clammy face of blood-shot eyes and running nose – had saddened her. She asked angrily, "Why, Angie?"

"Oh, Linda, give me some money, please! I can't stand it anymore." Angie outstretched a trembling hand.

"No, Angie, please don't touch that stuff again. It'll kill you. You need professional help. Go back to the Center, they can help you and may give you a job after you're healed."

"I can't quit and I don't want a lousy job!"

"Yes, you can."

"You really think it's that easy? How do you know? You've never got hooked before!" Angie was extremely agitated, screaming like a madwoman.

"I never got hooked because I'm not stupid," retorted Linda. But, right away she knew she had said the wrong thing. It is not the time to antagonize Angie; I should be supportive and sympathetic, and that was what Angie desperately needs right now, she reminded herself.

Seeing Angie's pale face turn crimson with anger, Linda quickly held Angie's hand and said, "I'm terribly sorry, my dear little sister, I didn't mean it. Be honest, if I hadn't feigned having allergic reaction to that stuff, I'm sure I'd have got hooked just like you had, and I'm not sure I could quit either. I'm smarter because I had learned it the hard way. In order to survive in the streets, I had to use my head. There was no one I could turn to for help. Not like you; you had your parents before you left home and have me afterward. I've always been taking care of you, haven't I?"

Angie did not answer and she did not explode any more either. Every word that Linda said was true and touching and they made Angie recall all the favors that Linda had done for her. She disengaged her hands from Linda's so she could embrace Linda tightly and cried out, "Help me, Big Sis, just this one more time. I'll check in the Center later when I feel better."

"No, you must check in tonight. Now! Go get ready, I'll be back to take you there," ordered Linda and she left to tell Randy and Rob.

TWENTY-ONE

A week later, Angie was discharged from the rehab center, but she didn't take the job offer. "Thank you for the offer, I'll think about it for a few days and let you know," Angie said to the director of the Center, using her usual excuse. She had already decided not taking the job because it paid so little and, besides, her dream of having her own business was still much alive in her head.

She came over to Randy's house one night to talk to Linda about their internet business. But, to her surprise Linda was not interest in it anymore; she seemed to like her new job very much. "I'm happy with my job, it doesn't pay much but the people at the restaurant are very nice to me," said Linda.

"How can you live on the lousy minimum wage?"

"With the tips I make enough to be comfortable, in fact, I manage to save some money every month because Uncle Randy doesn't let me pay for the rent and the food."

"That's very nice of him but the internet business we have been talking about will make us rich and you don't have to work that hard and have to put out a Goddamn smile for other people. Imagine, Linda, we'll have our own place, do whatever we want to do and don't have to be careful with this and careful with that. You know what I mean, do you? Living with two old people and have to do things according to their dumb rules is just too God-damn difficult."

"I know, but Uncle Randy won't like it."

"Why should we care he likes it or not, it is none of his Goddamn business, it's ours, Linda, our own!"

"But—but, if Uncle Randy doesn't like it, he must have his reason. You know, he's old and smart, he ought to know better than us."

"He, smart my ass, he's just another old fool who doesn't know what internet is and doesn't know how to use a smart phone, even a three-year-old knows how to use one. Believe me, all old people are stupid. Do you think you could clean up Old Sam's wallet if he was not old?"

Randy was in his bedroom reading when Angie came and he heard her and Linda were talking in the living room. At first, he wasn't paying any attention to their conversation; he ignored it as silly girl's talk. But as their discourse got louder and louder, he couldn't help but put down the book and started listening. The way Angie tried to persuade Linda to go into business with her and how freely they spoke with a lot of profanities had amused him enormously. But he had no intention to go into the living room and interrupt their conversation till he heard Angie call him "old fool" and "smart my ass." He was not angry though, he thought it would be a good opportunity to re-form the two juveniles, transforming them from hookers into two good girls.

"Hi girls, what are you two talking about this late?"

"Nothing much, Uncle Randy, we're just chattering a little." Horrified by Randy's unexpected appearance, the two girls replied simultaneously, they thought he went to bed already.

"Nothing uh, but I heard someone call me "old fool and smart my ass." Randy put on a serious face.

The girls now not only horrified but petrified also, their faces were flaming red and had no idea what to say. They wished, at that very moment, could find a hole to crawl in. Their awkward situation was made worse by Randy's sudden, perplexing outburst of laughter.

Still laughing, Randy ordered Linda to fetch the bottle of scotch – an expensive single malt whisky that Linda had bought for him for his birthday – and three glasses. Linda was more than happy to comply and she disappeared like a gopher. Anything was better than standing there, hanging her head, and having Uncle Randy's piercing eyes staring at her.

"Let's having a party tonight," said Randy gleefully after he poured everyone a shot. "We can talk about anything and we can argue as much as we want." Like magic his cheerful face disappeared and in its place appeared a serious one, and with a serious voice he continued, "But we must talk from our hearts, be honest and be respectful to each other, and no four-lettered words, please. We must talk and argue like a lady and a gentleman, okay girls?"

None of the girls said anything; they looked at each other for answers. Has Uncle Randy gotten too old and gone crazy? They asked in silence.

From the girls' baffled expressions, Randy realized his try-to-be-funny acts did not deliver the result he had intended, instead of relaxing them and creating a friendly atmosphere; it stiffened them further and put them in a very tense situation. "Hey, girls, loosen up! Cheer!" He raised his glass and signaled the girls to follow suit. They did and clinked glasses. "Now, what you girls want to talk about? We have a whole night ahead of us." Hearing no response from the girls, he suggested, "Oh, I know, how about the same subject you girls had been talking before I came out. Maybe you girls need some inputs from me."

"Yeah, let's talk to Uncle Randy; see what he thinks about it. Okay, Angie?" cried Linda excitedly. She had high hope that Randy could help her solve her problem –

the problem of unable to decide whether she should go into the internet business with Angie. The money and the freedom of owning a business was tempting, but somehow she felt it wasn't a good kind of business.

"I did already. Uncle Randy didn't like it!"

"You never told me that."

"Damn you, Linda, you always forgot!" Angie started getting uptight, the ugly confrontation with Randy at the park was still vivid in her mind, and Linda was a convenient scapegoat to release her anger.

"Sorry, I've forgotten."

Randy watched Angie thoughtfully with his thick eyebrows locked close together, and when he saw her hanging her head in silence, he finally said in the softest and kindest voice he could manage, for he remembered he had touched her hot-button twice already and did not want to do it again: "Angie, my dear, please watch your language and your temper. We can't discuss and solve anything if we get mad with each other so easily. I'm old and maybe foolish sometimes but I'm not a stubborn old fool. I consider myself quiet liberal and democratic. I listen to new ideas but I don't follow them blindly; I use my head to sort out what I should follow and what I shouldn't. Let us go back to your internet business and all the hot questions you'd thrown at me the other day. I'm sorry I did not have any good answers for you at the time because you gave me no chance; you were so mad and walked out on me. Do you know what I did after you left? I didn't get mad at you, I sat on the same park bench for more than two hours, thinking about your questions—."

"I'm sorry, I truly am." Angie apologized with regret.

"It is okay, dear. I was thinking about them, I mean your questions, day and night for a whole week and I think I've got the answers now. Do you girls care to hear why I oppose it?"

"We do, please." They both answered.

"Great! In that case, we better have your Daddy here, too. Do you mind, Angie, giving him a call and tell him I want him here?"

TWENTY-TWO

When Rob Taylor came, Randy poured him a half glass of the expensive scotch and said, "Rob, we've been talking about Linda and Angie's future and we want your participation. It'll be a long discussion and everyone is welcome to speak his mind, but we must talk in friendly terms, no yelling and no profanity, okay?"

"Fine with me," said Rob. And the girls said the same.

"Rob, I can't remember I've told you about Linda asking me for a loan to start an internet business."

"You had, something she called 'consoling services' for lonely people." I don't like it. It is disgusting!"

"I don't like it either. I remember I'd said to Linda, 'Why do you still want to be in the same filthy business, Linda?' You know what she said? She said, 'Why not, it makes more money than waiting tables. And, it's an easy job; I don't even have to leave the house.' Then, I said, 'But, it's a dirty business. No decent person doing it.' And then she said, 'I don't see it's dirty. We just provide services for the people who need them, just like doctors provide cares for their patients.' I was rather upset at that time by her dogmatic argument, so I shut her up. Sorry, Linda, I had lost my temper."

After pausing to take a sip of scotch, he continued cautiously, he had to be careful with the words he was going to use and the tone with which he was going to deliver them. "Here are the reasons for my objection," he said. "One, selling sex over the internet is illegal, you may go to jail for that. Two, it is immoral—."

"It isn't, lot of people doing it." Angie protested.

126

"Please let me finish first and wait for your turn, okay?" Randy kept his cool and continued, "Third, I don't think you have a future in it. You see, there is a lot of competition out there and you girls are not going to be young and attractive forever, people will get tired of talking and looking at the same girl. Now, I'm finished, it is your turn now. Girls, any question?"

Linda shook her head; she decided to sit on the fence watching from a distance the other three to fight it out. She had learned this trick long time ago at home and in the mean streets of Lake Eleazy. That was how she'd avoided getting into troubles and survived in the harsh environment.

But the contentious Angie had plenty of questions and she asked, "Uncle Randy, Do you mind to explain to us why selling sex is immoral, as Linda had said, we just provide a service that people need, like doctors, waitresses, teachers or whatever?"

"That's enough, Angie," shouted Rob, "here you go again. You haven't changed a bit."

Predicting a fight would soon erupt between father and daughter, and a disastrous split up would drive Angie back to Lake Eleazy again, Randy jumped in quickly to cool off the situation. He said, "Calm down, both of you. We can't solve problems by yelling at each other. Rob, do you mind be quiet for a while; I want to have a friendly discussion on this with the girls. Is it okay with you girls?"

"Fine, Uncle Randy," said Linda.

"What about you, Angie?" asked Randy.

"Fine," answered Angie lethargically.

"Good! Now remember, girls, we're here to solve problems as a family. So, please don't raise your voice.

Now, let me answer your question, Angie. Because good people consider sex is dirty and bad."

"All sex is dirty and bad? How about sex between a man and a woman, between two men, between two women, or a man by himself, and a woman by herself, are they all dirty and bad, too?"

These were tough questions, so appalling and bold that Linda stuck her tongue out in astonishment, and Randy was caught red-faced. He never expected Angie would have asked such embarrassing questions. He was speechless, searching urgently for an appropriate answer. But before he could find any, Rob scolded his daughter again, "Angie, you don't ask Uncle Randy such disgusting questions."

"It is all right, Rob," said Randy, regaining his composure. "To answer your questions, Angie, I'd say yes, except between a man and a woman."

"But, how come people condemn an unmarried couple for having sex, and in some countries, they will also be stoned to dead?"

"According to the Bible unmarried sex is a sin."

"God—God's Bible again, who wrote the God—Bible and how could he determine what's right and what's wrong?" Angie forced herself to *swallow* half of the word, Goddamn, when she suddenly remembered the request of her by Randy not to use profanity, but her concealment was poorly executed and Randy noticed it with a frown.

"I agreed with you on this, Angie. I've always questioned who is God if there is one at all, and what right he has to decide everything for us. That's why I'm an atheist. However, I believe open sex is wrong; it should be a private thing between two loving persons. That's the reason I object you girls selling sex over the internet or at street corners."

"Uncle Randy, you'd contradicted yourself. Only a minute ago you said having sex is all right between a man and a woman, and now you say between two loving persons. How about between two loving men or two loving women, are they all right, too?"

Randy Gibbs got caught red-faced again, but this time he didn't fumble. He was by now well prepared for surprises from these two street-smart girls. He said calmly, "Well, it's okay with me as long as they conduct their business discreetly and not to seduce, encourage or impose on other people to commit the same act. This is my opinion, of course, and I've told you that I'm a liberal."

"You also said that having sex openly is not acceptable. But, why it is all right with animals, insects and fish, they do it openly, don't they?"

"That's why they remain animals, insects and fish. But we're civilized human beings; we do things in a civilized way, the way that is acceptable to other people. If you do things that are unacceptable to other people, they will call you barbarians, savages, or animals."

"Who is "other people" anyway and why should I care they accept me or not?"

"You should, Angie, because "other people" is all the people besides you who live on this planet. If they don't accept you, you'll become an outcast and they'll make your life miserable. I think people who do unacceptable things are pretty dumb."

"Such as?"

"Like wearing provocative clothes and hairdos, tattooing, body-piercing, doing drugs, excessive drinking, or necking and fondling in public, are acceptable to you young people but not to us old folks."

Noticing Angie having an adversarial expression on her face, Randy asked her, "You want to say something, Angie?"

"Yes, Uncle Randy, are we young people always wrong and you old folks always right?"

At her question Rob was displeased, but he managed to sit still and keep quiet but with tremendous effort.

"No, Angie, I didn't say that. We all, young or old, have our rights and wrongs. Any old folk obstinately sticks to the old ways and blatantly rejects the new ways without giving them any considerations is a stupid old fool. By the same token, any youngster rejects the old ways as outdated, and adopts the new ways blindly without thinking is also a stupid fool. Right or wrong, all depends on the situation, the time, and the place. Sometimes, total honesty is wrong and a little lying is right; sometimes, nudity is okay and sometimes is not—"

"Can you be more specific, Uncle Randy?" Angie interrupted. "How about use dress and hairdo and tattoo as an example?"

"Good idea. Let's talk about dress first, say, an ordinary pair of pants and a shirt, which is perfectly okay for everyday casual wear, but is too casual for concert, wedding, or funeral. The same reasoning applies to wearing a suit to the park or beach. Do you remember, Angie, when you came to meet me at the restaurant wearing those sexy clothes, people stared at us as if we were pariahs. Be honest with you, Angie, I was extremely uncomfortable."

"Why should you?" Angie asked, perplexed.

"Don't you understand, from what you wore and how you walked and talked, people profiled you as a bad person, and they wondered what kind of business I had with you, of course, they didn't know I'm your uncle. You see, people judge a person by his/her appearance."

"I'm sorry I'd embarrassed you," said Angie.

"That's okay. You see how important it is for us to behave within the norm. Any behavior that is outside the norm will not be accepted by the general public, people will treat you negatively. You'll have a hard time finding a job or making friends, in short, a lot of doors will be closed to you."

"I can understand that, Uncle Randy," said Angie, "but why talking to a customer over the internet is a dirty job?"

"It all depends on what are you talking about. If you are talking about business or even weather, it's fine. But, if you are talking with your customers about sex, it is not. Well, I can see now what our problem is. It is that we have different opinion about things, especially between you young girls and us old men. It's understandable because we're born and raised a quarter of a century apart and, therefore, our backgrounds, traditions, experiences, and moral standards are very much different. All these have a huge influence on our thinking and opinions."

"But time has changed," Angie argued. "The old ways, old traditions, old moral standards and the old norms, which, I'm sure, had their merits during their times, must change too. They are no longer suitable for modern day living. For example: we don't wear the same style of clothes which was popular just twenty years ago, we don't have black-and-white TV in our homes and fax machines in our offices anymore, and we seldom write letters now, we use emails, texting, What Sapp, and Facebook to communicate with each other. Just to take a quick look, Uncle Randy, almost everything we touch has changed."

"Those changes are due to the changes in technology which makes things better and more efficient," said Rob

131

who thought he was more equipped than Randy to argue with Angie on these technological topics, because he was an engineer.

"There have been a lot of social changes, too, Daddy. Not too long ago, wearing suits and ties and leather shoes to the office was almost a must, now people wear tennis shoes and T-shirt to work, even you seldom wear suits now except on special occasions. Also, interracial marriage, homosexuality, tattooing, sex alteration, breast implants and even jazz music were treated as something weird; but now, thanks to the visionary pioneers and our heroes, they are not only acceptable but also very commonplace. Without their courageous demands for changes and justice we probably would have stayed in the eighteen century."

"You call those trouble-making protesters and activists pioneers and heroes?" They are the ones who'd turned this world upside down. They were the ones who'd turned Lake Eleazy, a peaceful fishing village, into a sinful town as it is now. They were the ones who'd turned you two girls into junkies and hookers..." His daughter had unearthed all the angers and frustrations Rob had accumulated during the past seven years; He had been blaming the demise of his daughter and the problems of his family on the bad influence of her friends, on the rock and roll music, violent movies, prevailing drug problems, leniency of the law, and the deterioration of morality as a whole.

Unexpectedly, the argument had shifted; it was now between daughter and father, which made Randy very nervous. With a liberal daughter and a conservative father talking politics is like putting a lion and a tiger in the same cage, all you need to induce a fight is to throw them a piece of meat. He worried it would be getting too hot to handle, and he was looking urgently for opportunities to take over the debate again.

"It isn't fair to say that, Daddy, protesters are the catalysts of social change, without them we would've been as primitive as our ancestors of thousands of years ago. They do society a service and make our lives better."

"Better my foot!" Rob cried. "Look, they make things unequal with affirmative action and equal pay, they make us line up to pee with those unisex restrooms, they shut us up with political correctness. Every time we voice our opinions they will accuse us either racist or sexists. They can say anything they want but we can't. They have the right of free speech but we only have the right to be silent! You know how many good men and their families got ruined just because some irresponsible women accusing them sexual harassments? Although the accusers have no proof and their allegations may not be true, the accused got punished all the same by getting fired or being forced to resign. The irony is that there is no penalty for false accusers; they can get away with murders!"

Overwhelmed by her father's dominating voice, Angie was wordless, and while she was searching for a rebuttal, Randy seized this rare opportunity to break up the looming fight and veer from the subject by saying, "Sorry, Rob, I must say I have to be with Angie on this one. Protesters and activists are visionaries and heroes; they sacrifice themselves for all of us, without them nothing would have changed. Though not all changes are good, a lot of them are and necessary and we should welcome them. Perhaps, someday prostitution will be accepted as one of the normal businesses just like restaurants. Now, let's get back to our main discussion; we've been drifting too far from it. Politics is too touchy a subject, too complicated and divergent for ordinary folks like us to understand. Now, let's not wasting our time arguing about things that we have no control, we should focus on things that are really important to us. But, before we continue, I suggest we take a break first; it is almost midnight now and I'm hungry. Linda, how about making some peanut butter and jelly sandwiches and I'll brew a pot of coffee, I think we need it to stay awake."

TWENTY-THREE

After taking a brief break for their midnight snacks, Randy gave Linda and Angie a serious look as he said, "Now, you two listen carefully, we're going to discuss your internet business, the one you girls call 'Consoling Services'. I must be honest with you. I don't like it and I tell you why. Because it won't be accepted by our society, wait, Angie, I know what you want to say. You want to say: who care! Is that right?"

Angie nodded.

Randy continued, "You should, Angie, because our society decides what is right and acceptable and what is not. I know you'll ask what right our society has can make such important decision for us. You see, it is the same principle as voting: majority wins and that is minority has to follow majority. It really has nothing to do with right or wrong, which by itself has no meaning at all, as I said before, without the reference to situation, time and place. The rights of yesterday could be the wrongs of today, and today's rights could be tomorrow's wrongs. By the same theory, what is right here in our society may not be right in other societies, or vice versa."

Noticing Linda's baffled face and Angie's moving around impatiently in her seat with frustration, Randy knew he had been preaching Bible to Amazon jungle natives. He corrected himself hastily by saying, "Okay girls, let me give you an example: say, interracial marriage. By itself it is neutral, neither right nor wrong. But only half a century ago it was off-limit, interracial-married couples were stared at with contempt and their mixed children were called derogatorily 'bastards'. They were the outcasts of the society. But now, interracial marriage is very common and nobody raise an eyebrow at them anymore. You see, When the society accept it, it is right, otherwise, it is wrong, as simple as that. You girls understand?"

This time, both girls nodded.

"Good!' Randy said with a smile, "I won't be surprised if prostitution will one day be accepted by society just like any other legitimate business. Be honest with you, I don't see anything wrong with it myself, but I am against it because our society is against it. Too bad our society is not accepting prostitution at this time; otherwise, I would have no problem with what you gals want to do. Of course, you can go against the society and do something unacceptable, but you will be punished for it just like those interracial-married couples had been punished by their society in those days. You know, I love you both very much and I don't want to see you gals get hurt, and I respect whatever decisions you make for yourself. If you strongly believe in your internet business and want to sacrifice yourself for those lonely, hungry men, you may go ahead. You have the right to do so, so have I to look after my own interest first, to protect my good reputation, for which I'd spent a lifetime to build, from getting ruined overnight by two hooker nieces. Let me put it more bluntly: I have the right not to let you live in my house and call me 'Uncle'. You may think I'm selfish and old-fashioned. Yes, I am. I think of myself and my family and the people I love first; I refuse to put myself in a position where I stand out like a sore thumb, I have to go with the flow of other people and be accepted and respected by them. Life is much easier and more enjoyable that way. I hope you two understand."

For a long time there was total silence in the living room although the lights in there were still burning brightly. Nobody uttered a word but all wore a solemn face. Randy's speech was just too touching and powerful for them not to have an emotional disturbance. Linda broke the silence first, she got off her seat and came over to embrace Randy from the back and said, "I understand why we were wrong now, Uncle. Thank you for loving me and giving me a wonderful home, thank you, thank you…" Angie was next. She did the same thing, to Randy first then her father, and did it earnestly. Rob was last, he got up to refill everybody's glass and proposed a toast, "Cheers, one big happy family again!"

TWENTY-FOUR

At the rehab center Angie Taylor was doing great; she not only had kicked off the awful addiction but also had accepted the job offer as an assistant motivator and later on as an assistant counselor to the director himself. The director, who saw the potential in Angie, kept her very busy with the responsibility of training and counseling other drug addicts. As he had predicted, she did a wonderful job; she was so interested in helping other addicts to get off drug that she had developed friendships with many of them. She saw her former self in them and realized how sad it was to be an addict. Only then, she declared war on drug and decided to devote herself to help as many patients as she could.

At home she was doing equally well; she got along fine with her father now, more than fine actually, it was better than ever before. They conversed often, sharing stories about her new job and the addicts under her care. She finally found a meaningful purpose to live, at home as well as at work.

As with Linda and Randy, Angie treated her like a sister and him, an uncle. They had dinners together most of the time, either at Rob's home or at Randy's or at restaurants; they travelled far and near together; and they did a lot of other things as a close-knitted family. Happy as they were, there was still one thing remained unsettled: Rob Taylor and the two girls were living like ghosts. They conducted their daily businesses secretly and stealthily to avoid getting in contact with friends and neighbors. Rob was still reluctant to join his circle of friends at the Stagecoach Inn for breakfast, and Angie and

Linda had to sneak in and out of Rob and Randy's house like mice. In the eyes of his friends and neighbors, except Randy, Rob still remained a beggar and his daughter, a hooker, and Linda, a mysterious girl came from nowhere and her relationship with Randy was a favorite topic for gossips.

This awkward situation could have been easily ignored if not for Randy, who wanted to use the bitter-sweet story of Angie and Rob Taylor to teach their friends and neighbors a good lesson. He planned to throw a surprise party for them during which he would tell the touching story of the Taylor family, and using the occasion to formally introduce the two former hookers into their new neighborhood. But he had to wait until the time when he was absolutely sure that Angie's drug problem was over. It would be a huge embarrassment for them all if she got addicted again after the party.

It had been almost three months since Angie came home, during which scandalous rumors about two mysterious girls had been swirling about the neighborhood like pollens in spring. Unspoken questions and watchful eyes had made both Rob and Randy uncomfortable, if not unbearable. At that point Randy had decided that the time he had been waiting for had finally arrived, but, to be on the safe side, he went to have a talk with the director of the rehab center, who had assured him that Angie had fully recovered and her chance of a relapse was zero.

With the director's assurance, Randy proposed a surprise party that night after dinner.

"Hurrah! Is it your birthday party, Uncle?" asked Linda gleefully, to which Randy did not answer but smiled surreptitiously.

"Isn't it great, Angie, you and I can dance? We haven't been to a party for a long time now and I miss dancing," said Linda. But to her bewilderment, Angie was quiet and her response was lukewarm.

"What's the matter, Angie? I know you love parties."

"Not anymore," answered Angie indifferently and she looked melancholic.

"Why?"

"Why? How can I face Daddy's friends and neighbors? They all know I was a drug addict and a hooker."

"Ha, ha, ha," laughed Randy suddenly. He had been acting strangely while the two girls were nattering, as if he had something to surprise them. "I throw a party to embarrass them not you, Angie."

"What? Uncle Randy, please don't play game with us!" exclaimed both girls simultaneously. Only Rob was drinking his coffee silently, smiling. He knew what kind of party it would be and its purpose. Randy had told him.

"You see, Angie," Randy began, "some of our friends and neighbors aren't true friends and neighbors. When they found out you were a hooker and your father a beggar, they aren't friendly and neighborly anymore. They gossip about you and your father and show no sympathy. Since we now know who they are, we're going to teach them a lesson. And for those who have been helpful and supportive, we must show our appreciation. More importantly, I want to tell them what a great father your father is. To rescue you from prostitution and drug addiction, he was willing to suffer the pain of being disgraced and abused, and the torture and humiliation of panhandling at street corners. I also want to tell them what two tough girls you and Linda are, who had not only survived the mean streets of Lake Eleazy, but also had the courage and determination to pull yourselves out of a hellish trap. Angie, Linda, I'm very proud of you both. I truly am."

Overwhelmed with emotion, Linda turned around and threw herself into Randy's arms and cried, "Oh, Daddy, I love you very, very much!" Then, she kissed him on the cheek multiple times until he pushed her away embarrassingly but gently. Her act was spontaneous and genuine for she had been touched deeply by his praise. Nobody had ever praised her before. Randy was the first one.

"I love you too, honey," said Randy as he was caressing his crying baby awkwardly.

Equally powerful, but in a different way, was Uncle Randy's praise on Angie; it had helped her to make up her mind to stay sober and drug-free. Any misstep in the wrong direction would surely be a big disappointment for both her father and Uncle Randy. She would never forgive herself for hurting them again after having seen how proud they were of her.

"Thank you very much for your kind words. I promise you I won't disappoint you again," said Angie sincerely. "But as to the party, I don't think it's necessary. As long as we're happy as a family, let people talk, let them do what they want. Why should we care? Why should you spend the money to teach them a lesson? They may not learn anything anyway."

"Angie my dear, we should care what our friends and neighbors think of us, because they are the society, don't forget that. If we think their opinions of us are incorrect, we must try our best to correct them. It is our responsibilities."

"But it's not fair for you to pay for the party, Uncle Randy, you've done enough already. Let Linda and I pay, okay?"

"No, Angie, I'll pay for the party," said Rob. "How can we be so ungrateful not show our appreciation for what Uncle Randy has done for us? How can we not telling our friends and neighbors that you have changed and now my dear daughter again? How can we not to announce to the world that Linda has finally found a father who truly loves her? And how can Randy and I not letting people know how proud and happy we are to have both of you home? Oh, Randy, please tell them our plan. They need to know so they can prepare for the party."

TWENTY-FIVE

Naturally, the party was held at Stagecoach Inn for two simple reasons: first, it was a home-away-from-home for Rob and Randy and most of their friends and neighbors who had spent a lot of time congregating there for breakfast and afternoon coffee. Secondly, the cafeteria was inexpensive and served no alcoholic beverage. Obnoxious and disruptive behavior induced by alcohol was a major concern for the kind of party Randy intended to host.

Randy, the self-appointed host, sent out the invitations in which he clearly indicated that it would be a surprise party and no gifts would be accepted. That caused puzzlement for all invitees, for Randy had never had a party before besides, perhaps, his own wedding. But nobody knew for sure because when they knew him he had already been married. And everybody knew that he did not believe in celebrating birthday and wedding anniversary.

The party was an early buffet dinner, nothing fancy but plenty of food and drinks. It would be a casual and comfortable party. There were no sight of Rob, Angie or Linda; they were waiting outside in Randy's car to be introduced according to their plan. Randy was the only one to play the affable host, greeting guests and directing them to their seats, and he did an amazing job, for all of them were either old neighbors or old friends.

When there was no more guest coming, Randy went up to the make-shift stage, which was hastily put together with a plank on two used tires, and he calmly picked up the microphone and addressed the crowd: "Dear Friends and Neighbors, you may have been wondering what kind of surprise party this is. Before I tell you, I want you to guess. I bet you nobody will guess it right."

"Your birthday party," someone shouted.

"Nope, I've never celebrated my birthday and never will. I don't believe I should be happy on the day when my mother was suffering the most."

People were astounded. What a crazy idea, some thought. But, when they gave it a little more thought they found it make a lot of sense.

"Anniversary?" someone asked timidly.

"Nope, just like Birthday, I don't celebrate because I don't want to be reminded every year the biggest mistake I've ever made."

Mistake! What is he talking about? Marriage is a mistake? Some people wondered whether Randy was insane or disoriented by the medication he was taking. Only a few, whose marriages were total failures, understood what he meant, but they didn't understand why he would have said that, for he seemed to have a great marriage. They were all mystified and no one dared to ask him for an explanation.

"It must be your engagement party," said Jay Jensen's wife, standing up and smiling, very sure of herself because one of Randy's neighbors had told her that a young lady went in and out of Randy's house recently.

"No, no, no, Joanne," denied Randy, laughing, thinking she must be joking. "I'm too old for that. Besides, who'd want to marry an old stick like me, anyway?"

Amid thunderous laughter, Joanne sat down reluctantly, defiant and embarrassed; she couldn't accept she was wrong. Had her husband not pulled her down and hushed her, she would have disclosed the name of the informer.

"Anyone else?" Randy asked.

"Farewell party," shouted one of the old-timers who had noticed recently that Randy seemed to be preoccupied with something else.

"Nope, I'm not dying or going anywhere." His humorous reply aroused another round of laughter.

After the noisy crowd had quieted down, Randy continued, "I assume nobody knows the answer. Now, let me tell you. This party has, not one, not two, but three surprises. The first surprise is for a great father who disguised as a poor beggar, panhandling in the vicinity where his hooker daughter worked in order to save her from the miserable life of drug and prostitution. He had to put up with dirty clothes and unkempt appearance, which is difficult for a normally neat and clean person. He had to swallow his pride and endure the humiliation from those who threw some loose changes into his tin cup. He had to suffer the pains of being deserted and ridiculed by old friends and old neighbors."

By now, most guests knew the person Randy was referring to was Rob Taylor. Who else had a hooker daughter and who else was seen begging at Three Corner in Lake Eleazy? Whispers began to spread from head to head and from table to table, and it didn't take long to fill the whole restaurant. Only those disloyal neighbors and friends were quiet, among them were Jay Jensen and his wife. Remorse and guilt and shame had slipped through the cracks into their conscience and started making them uneasy in their seats. They all hung their heads and stared at the floor, looking for a hole to hide, like guilty defendants waiting for verdicts.

"And most painful of all," continued Randy. "He couldn't tell people the truth because he felt shameful to have a daughter like that. Be honest, how many of us have the courage and unconditional love to sacrifice ourselves like him? Probably none! My dear friends and neighbors, please welcome Rob Taylor back from his self-sacrificing journey."

Following Randy's hand, people turned around and saw Rob entering the restaurant. He walked steadily, nodding and smiling at people as he went passing them toward the stage amid thunderous clapping of hands. He looked like a beggar no more but a fastidious engineer; dressed exactly like the Rob Taylor whom his friends and neighbors knew so well. When he got on the stage and faced the cheering crowd, he said, "I'm embarrassed, Randy gave me too much credit. He should deserve all the credits; without him my daughter will be still standing at Three Corner of Lake Eleazy, and I'll be still locking myself up at home and drinking my sorrow away. I was depressed and had no desire to live. He got me out of deep depression and spent days if not weeks to persuade me to go along with his plan to save my daughter, Angie. You know, to be a beggar, even it was only acting, was very difficult for me, but Randy was so insistent. Looking back it was entirely my fault; I should have asked for help but I was too proud to ask. How could you help if you didn't know I need help? Now, I'm no longer a beggar and my daughter no longer a hooker, may I ask you, our friends and neighbors, be generous and kind to her, forget what she was and treat her by what she is now. Thank you."

After Rob finished, Randy took over the microphone, "My next surprise is the princess of a loving family, who unfortunately turned into a runway, a drug addict, a porn star and a hooker. But with her own courage and tenacity she dug her way out of the fire pit to become a totally different person. Not only she is drug-free now, she also has a great job at a rehab center as an assistant counselor, helping other addicts to get off the dreadful addiction.

146

You have no idea how difficult it is to accomplish what she had accomplished without going through what she had gone through. She is our hero. Friends and Neighbors, please welcome Angie Taylor, our new princess."

Just like her father, Angie appeared and walked gracefully to the stage, wearing no provocative clothes or outrageous makeups and accessories; only a conservative white blouse and a dark grey skirt and a pair of black low heels. Still, she was provoking, made possible by her beauty, by the graceful way she walked, by the dignified smiles and nods she bestowed on people who applauded and welcomed her, and by the penetrating and intense stares at those who did not. When she stepped on the stage, she gave Uncle Randy and her father an affectionate hug before her speech. "Thank you very much for your kind words, Uncle Randy," began Angie. "You're the one who deserves the most credit. Without your help and Daddy's love, I wouldn't be here today. You'd made my return from the journey to hell possible, and you'd saved my life. For that I'm forever grateful. Now that I realize how loving and comfortable our home is that I have to admit I was a fool when I ran away from it. I'm not making excuses for myself; but I was young then and I was spoiled by my parents who gave me too much love and not enough guidance and discipline. I got used to doing thing my way without having to face the consequence, and I took everything for granted. When my parents didn't give me what I wanted, I took it as if they didn't love me anymore and I'd feel hurt and get angry and become rebellious. Like any rebellious child I wanted to get back at my parents, to hurt them. And the only way to hurt them was to hurt myself, because I knew they loved me very much, and nothing could hurt them more than seeing me getting hurt. But, I was in pain, too, to know that they were in pain—I—I guess I still loved them…" Angie's voice trailed off to a halt before she retrieved a handkerchief to dry her eyes. Many old ladies followed suit, for they had been holding back their tears for a while. As mothers themselves, they could feel Angie's pain much deeper than the men could, perhaps with the exception of her father who disguised his womanly act by blowing his nose loudly and by wiping a little bit higher than his nose. "It sounds silly," resumed Angie. "It didn't take me long to realize I'd made a big mistake after having to face the evil streets of Lake Eleazy. I regretted I'd left home, but I couldn't go back although I knew my parents would've welcome me back. Juvenile pride had prevented me. I wanted to prove them wrong about me and I wanted to show them I could make it in this world on my own, regardless what price I had to pay. That was how I got into the shameful business.

After I dug myself deeper and deeper into my grave and knew that it was no way out, I gave up all hopes and didn't care I die or live. But, very strangely, when Linda told me my father was begging at Three Corner, I was in pain and shameful at the same time, and I wanted to help him financially so he didn't have to beg. I didn't know why then, but I know now. It was the undying love between a child and its parents. And it was the same undying love that made my father willingly become a beggar in order to save me. My father wasn't broke and he didn't have to be a beggar. The whole thing was thought up by our clever next-door neighbor, Uncle Randy, who also recruited my good friend, Linda, to help saving me.

"At that time, I'd fallen too low and was too shameful of myself to expect a new beginning was possible. But Linda helped me make up my mind; she insisted to stay behind with me if I refused to go home, even though she was very excited about Uncle Randy's offer – to help her find a job and let her stay in his house. You know, I love Linda; she is my best friend and almost like a sister to me, I just couldn't bear to ruin her future because of me. Linda is my schoolmate and friend, she is the one who got me into trouble by introducing me to her circle of bad friends, but she is also the one who helped me getting out of it. She had protected me from all sorts of bad people and had guided me navigating the mean streets of Lake Eleazy. Without her, I'm sure I wouldn't have survived that kind of hostile environment. Linda, where are you? Come on out. Here she's," she cried out, pointing at a person sitting at the back row near the entrance. "Linda, please come here, I want to introduce you to our friends and neighbors."

Linda, wearing a Stagecoach Inn uniform, walked briskly to the stage and when she was on it, Angie announced, "Here's my best friend, Linda. Let's give her a hand." Angie led an overwhelming applause which took her a while to quiet it down. After that she continued, "Linda is much smarter than I; she never got hooked with drug as I did and always wanted to get out of that dirty business. Now, we both have jobs and we're very happy. Dear friends and neighbors, you can make us happier by forgetting our past and allowing us a chance to live a normal life. Thank you all very much."

"Angie, you've spoiled my fun. Now, everybody knows what my third surprise is," said Randy. "Well, all the same, you'll be surprised if I tell you Linda isn't my bride as Mrs. Jensen has speculated. She is my daughter!"

Uproar of disbelief filled the restaurant instantly and all the old-timers with whom Randy had breakfast regularly dropped their jaws almost to the floor. They all knew

149

he and his wife did not have any children. Where this daughter of his came from? They wondered.

"Let me explain," said Randy quickly. "Linda is a good friend of Angie who sent her to see me about her father. After talking to her I found out she is a nice girl who had run away from home when she was only thirteen, because her stepfather had sexually abused her. I felt sorry for her so I recruited her to help saving Angie, and I promised her I'll let her live in my house and get her a job. You know what; we fell in love with each other, not as lovers, of course, but as father and daughter. The only regret we have is that we didn't meet earlier and Edith is not here to share our happiness. One more thing I want to surprise you: both girls are doing great. Linda is working now at this restaurant and getting along well with everybody here. Angie is working at the rehab center as an assistant counselor, trying to save other addicts. I'm very proud of them and I think you all should because it isn't easy to accomplish what they had accomplished. Now, Linda, do you have anything to say to us?"

"I do," answered Linda. "I just want everybody to know how lucky I am to have a father who truly loves me. You may not believe me, before I met him I didn't know what love is. My own father, who was a gambler and an alcoholic, abandoned us when I was three and my two step-fathers, one ignored me and the other sexually abused me. My poor mother, who was a nervous wreck, had too many husbands and children and too busy to have any time left for me. Growing up in such an environment, I became hateful and distrustful and a little smarter, too. When Daddy first offered me help, I said to myself: this dirty old man is up to something, I better watch out for him—"

150

"Your time is up, Linda," Randy cut in quickly lest her loose tongue spit out something inappropriate. "We better wrap up the party and let the restaurant get ready for its dinner business.

TWENTY-SIX

At Stagecoach Inn the next day, Randy and Rob showed up together, a little late, and most regular old-timers had already been there waiting. They knew Rob would come because Randy had promised them the day before at the party that he'd bring Rob along regardless he liked it or not. It had been more than six months since last time Rob was there and he felt strangely uncomfortable when he walked pass the familiar door, but he held his head high, half a head higher than normal, and making confident strides. He received a genuine welcome; one by one the old-timers came to shake his hands, congratulate him for having his daughter back, and thank him for inviting them to his marvelous party. Even Jay Jenson came to do the same. He was a lot less noisy now and much humbler. Randy thought he had learned his lesson well. But nobody mentioned the speeches at the party, which was just what Rob and Randy wanted; they wanted to forget what had happened during the last six months. They wanted to have their ole good time back at their favorite place, Stagecoach Inn.

Watching Rob for the first time dominating the conversation, eagerly telling his story as a panhandler as if it was the most exciting job he ever had, Randy felt very proud of his best friend and of himself. He couldn't help but congratulate *himself* silently: Congratulation Randy! You've just saved three lives, two doomed hookers and one depressed man. Great job, Randy! Well done!

Made in the USA
Las Vegas, NV
04 September 2021